Love Shouldn't Hurt 3

Lock Down Publications and Ca$h
Presents

Love Shouldn't Hurt 3

A Novel by *Meesha*

Lock Down Publications
P.O. Box 870494
Mesquite, Tx 75187

Visit our website @
www.lockdownpublications.com

First Edition Mach 2019
Printed in the United States of America

Lock Down Publications
Like our page on Facebook: Lock Down Publications @
www.facebook.com/lockdownpublications.ldp
Cover design and layout by: **Dynasty Cover Me**
Book interior design by: **Shawn Walker**
Edited by: **Tisha Andrews**

Stay Connected with Us!

Text **LOCKDOWN** to 22828 to stay up-to-date with new releases, sneak peaks, contests and more…
Thank you.

Submission Guideline.

Submit the first three chapters of your completed manuscript to ldpsubmissions@gmail.com, subject line: Your book's title. The manuscript must be in a .doc file and sent as an attachment. Document should be in Times New Roman, double spaced and in size 12 font. Also, provide your synopsis and full contact information. If sending multiple submissions, they must each be in a separate email.

Have a story but no way to send it electronically? You can still submit to LDP/Ca$h Presents. Send in the first three chapters, written or typed, of your completed manuscript to:

LDP: Submissions Dept
Po Box 870494
Mesquite, Tx 75187

DO NOT send original manuscript. Must be a duplicate.

Provide your synopsis and a cover letter containing your full contact information.

Thanks for considering LDP and Ca$h Presents.

Dedication

Happy Heavenly birthday, Ladybug! Here's to another birthday that I will celebrate for the both of us! Oh how I wish I could hear you tell me happy birthday one more time. I love and miss you every day, but I know you are guiding me through ever second of my life. Well, on a happier note, I've done it again! Even though you knew that already. You have always cheered me on in whatever I was destined to achieve and you are still my cheerleader from above. I love you, Lady.

Martha L. Turner
3/19/1939-6/11/2015

Author's Note

This series is based on real life emotional events. I wrote it to capture just that...your emotions. There are parts of these books that bring awareness to situations that many won't or don't like to talk about. But the awareness in each book is relatable to someone out there. Thank you all so much for supporting me and I hope you enjoy *Love Shouldn't Hurt 3* as much as I enjoyed writing it.

Chapter 1
Drayton

Kaymee was the last person I expected to see while I was basically finger fucking Alexis' ass. I wasn't expecting her to kiss me, but when her lips connected to mine, the only thing I could think about was the mind-blowing sex we had the last couple of days. Getting lost in her kiss, I didn't come back to my senses until I heard Kaymee scream my name.

"Dray, what the fuck is going on?"

Looking like a child that got caught with their hand in the cookie jar, I was stuck for a minute until I saw her walk off in a huff. My first instinct was to go after her but when I started following her, Alexis grabbed me by the arm and let the cat out the bag. I wanted to knock her muthafuckin' teeth down her throat when she let the words she spoke come out of her mouth.

"I know damn well you are not fucking with another bitch! Not after the last couple of days we just had. Dray, what happened to 'it's me and you forever'?" she asked with an attitude, while holding me by the arm.

I couldn't blame her for saying the shit because I never let it be known that I had a woman. Ignoring Kaymee for damn near a week was fucked up, but the way Jonathan tried to check me pissed me off. I took my anger out on the wrong person and used Alexis to take my mind off the situation, another bad move.

"Alexis, this ain't the time for this! Let my fuckin' arm go!" I said, snatching away from her.

"You didn't have all this attitude when your dick was massaging my damn uterus, nigga! Who the fuck is she, Dray?" she snapped. The muthafuckas standing around was making a fiasco over the corny shit she said, nosy fucks.

"Who she is ain't your concern, so don't worry your mind about her. I'm gon' say this one time and one time only, stay away from her," I retorted and walked away from her to find Kaymee.

It took me a minute to figure out what direction she went in. As I looked around, I spotted her and Poetry walking fast in the parking lot. Heading that way, I heard someone coming up on me fast as fuck. I turned around and was face to face with Monty. The fire in his eyes were too defined to be missed. I knew he was pissed because his nostrils flared like a gorilla protecting his family.

"What the fuck did we discuss before we got back down here, Dray? I thought you had this shit under control, at least that's what the fuck you had me believing. Mee is not about to be around this bitch worrying about how many hoes you got. I don't care what you do. Just leave her the fuck out of it. She's been through enough shit back in Chicago. That's the reason she wanted to leave. If you ain't gon' do right, stay the fuck away from her because I'm letting you know now, I will fuck you up! Don't ever think about bringing no bitch to the crib, or you will get your ass whooped."

"Monty, have I ever told you what to do as far as your relationship? Nah, I haven't, so stay the fuck out of what me and Kaymee got going on. Last time I checked, she's grown and can make her own decisions. I would appreciate if you give me the same respect with my girl as I give you with yours."

"Nigga, this ain't no muthafuckin' random bitch! You got me fucked up if you think I'm about to sit around while you fuck over her. Get ya shit together because this right here will end the friendship we've built the last couple of years. You heard what the fuck I said. Let me see one muthafuckin' tear on her face over yo' ass. I'm gon' leave it at that," he said, walking off.

Monty couldn't say shit to me about what was going on. This was the same nigga that had a whole bitch while he was in a relationship. The difference between us was I wasn't losing my bitch behind this shit. His ass knew how I was before he introduced me to Kaymee. If he gave a fuck about her, he would've told her to run when she met me. I said what needed to be said to get where I wanted to be with her.

I glanced across the parking lot and Kaymee was standing by her truck talking to Poetry. I jogged over and Poetry looked up at me with a grimace on her face. I knew she was going to have something to say, so I was willing to let her get it out without snapping.

"Kaymee, let me talk to you for a minute, just the two of us," I said, grabbing her arm.

"Why do we have to go somewhere secluded?" she asked, snatching away almost hitting me in the face with the cast on her arm. "You weren't trying to hide when that bitch was all on your dick! Better yet, were you trying to be private when you had your thumb in her ass? How about when you had your fuckin' tongue down her throat? Fuck you, Dray! There's nothing to talk about. Nobody in Atlanta knows about us, but the one person that knows you oh so well is you! Don't think I didn't hear what she said. It explains why you wasn't answering any of my calls."

"It wasn't even like that, Kaymee. We were just dancing and she kissed me, catching me off guard."

"Get the fuck out of here with that bullshit! I guess kissing her back was just a reaction too, huh? I will not let her be stupid for your slick ass," Poetry spit out before Kaymee could reply.

“Poetry, mind yo’ business! This don’t have shit to do with you. This is between me and Kaymee. Go find Monty and argue about y’all shit. Stay the fuck outta this right here,” I said, moving my finger back and forth between Kaymee and myself.

“Monty and I may be going through some shit, but I’ll bet money if I text him and tell him you over here talking greasy, he’ll come in a heartbeat and swell your ass up! Don’t get an attitude with me because you got caught in a compromising position. And for the record, she is my muthafuckin’ business, nigga!”

“Poe, sit in the car for me, please. Let me talk to him,” she said, practically begging Poe to get in the car. “I’ll be ready to go afterwards.”

Shaking her head, Poetry glared at me while backing up. “One of these days you are gonna stop making excuses for his ass,” she turned to walk to the truck, while Kaymee watched.

When she turned and gave me her full attention, I saw the hurt etched on her face. She stood with her arms crossed, waiting for me to speak. I didn’t know what to say about the shit she’d witnessed, but I knew I didn’t want her to leave without me still being her man.

“I’m sorry, baby. There’s nothing going on with me and that girl. I will admit we used to fuck around, but that’s been dead. When I told you that I loved you, I meant what I said. There isn’t anything that will come between the two of us, I promise.”

I saw the longing in her eyes for me to be telling the truth, but her body language wanted to turn and walk away for good. “Tell me this. Were you with her a couple days ago?”

Sighing lowly, I stared in her eyes and told a bold-faced lie. "I saw her a couple days ago but that was just in passing at the gas station. She is a drama queen and she don't want to see me with anyone else. Alexis—she will say whatever she thinks will cause conflict. Don't believe shit she says, baby. It's me and you just like back in Chicago. Nothing has changed," I said, grabbing her around the waist. I bent down to kiss her and she stepped back quickly.

"You got this shit all wrong if you think you are about to put your mouth on me after kissing that bitch! Keep your hands off me. My skin is allergic to other people's ass remnants. That's nasty. You must be out of your mind. I don't believe none of that shit. Your actions told me what you didn't. Call me when you're ready to stop playing games with my fuckin' feelings," she said, turning to walk away.

I wasn't expecting her to come at me like she did and it angered me. All I knew was the timid and scared Kaymee. This was a side I'd never encountered and I didn't like it. I needed her ass to go back to the "yes girl" that I met months ago. That side of her was more controllable and I needed her to know who the fuck held the reign.

Stopping her in her tracks, I asked, "What does that mean, holla at you when I'm done playing games? This ain't a Poetry and Monty situation. Don't let her put that shit in your head. The shit that work with that nigga don't remotely work for me. To be honest, it would get you knocked upside your muthafuckin' head, Kaymee. That pussy is mine. It was fit to size one nigga, me. There will be no parting ways. Won't be no ignoring me like I'm a sap.

When I call, you better answer. Whenever I say come, you better break your neck to get wherever I am. There will be no questioning me about anything I do, the only thing you need to concentrate on is what I tell you to do and not do.

I'm gon' let you leave with Poe, but that is the last time you get the opportunity to tell me what you gon' do. Are we understood on that?"

I hated to treat her that way, but I saw the look she gave and I knew she was about to try to end shit. The only way we would split was when I decided I didn't want her ass no more, and I wasn't done with her yet. If putting fear in her ass was the way to make her see things my way, then so be it. She started biting at her nails, looking nervous and shit. I stood waiting on her to respond, but she didn't reply.

"Did you hear what the fuck I just said? Are we clear about it?" I asked, stepping in her face.

"Okay, I heard you, Dray," she said visibly shaken.

"One more thing, bet not nan muthafucka come to me about what the fuck I said either. If that shit happens, you will regret opening your mouth. Get out of here and go home. Welcome to the college life," I said, smirking at her as she rushed to get in the truck.

Chapter 2
Poetry

When Dray walked toward us, I wanted to grab Mee by her arm and go in the other direction, but it wasn't my fight. He stepped out his body talking about the shit wasn't my business. Anything that had to do with her was my damn business. He would learn that real soon. She asked me to wait in the truck while she talked to his punk ass and I did just that hoping she handled his ass accordingly.

I watched the entire interaction through the side mirror and I didn't like what I was seeing. The words weren't clear enough for me to hear, but her body language told me that shit was not right. Not only that, he stepped in her personal space and she all but jumped out of her body. I knew at that point I was going to have to keep my eye on his ass. His other side was making an appearance slowly.

There was no way Kaymee shouldn't have been cussing his ass out and leaving his ass looking stupid. That's what he did to her when he was damn near having sex with that girl in the middle of a crowd. What he was doing was unacceptable and to make matters worse, she saw the shit with her own eyes. She didn't have to wait for the shit to come out the shadows. She got slapped with it up close and personal.

Making sure she didn't leave my line of vision, I saw her shoulders slump more with every word spoken to her. Then his nasty ass had the nerve to try to kiss her. I'm glad she was smart enough not to allow that shit. She attempted to walk off and she stopped abruptly and turned back around. At that moment, I wished I was an ant on the ground because I needed to know what the fuck he said to her. She was wringing her hands like she was scared to death.

When she finally made her way to the truck, it was as if she was speed walking. I watched her until she opened the door and when she got in, she had tears in her eyes. Giving her time to gather herself, I patiently waited as I watched him walk away. I didn't like how defeated she looked. It reminded me of the days when Dot treated her like shit. He said something foul to her, but I didn't know what that something was.

"Talk to me, friend. What happened?"

"Nothing. Just take me back to my daddy's house."

Her voice cracked and a tear slid down her cheek. I couldn't let the day go to shit because of his slimy ass. "Kaymee, tell me what he said. I'm not trying to have another episode like the ones we had with Dot. You know you can talk to me about anything and that includes Dray."

She shook her head back and forth and continued to cry. I reached in the glove compartment and grabbed a couple napkins that were inside. Handing them to her, she wiped her face and calmed down a little bit. She turned her head and stared at the car that was parked next to us just to avoid talking about what was going on.

"We are not leaving. We came to have a good time and that's what we're going to do." Looking down at my phone, I checked to see what time it was. It was a quarter to seven. "There will be a concert in the main gym at seven thirty. We can leave as soon as it's over. I want to go because our girl Cardi B is going to be in the building along with the Migos. We've been waiting to see her in concert forever. Here's our chance and it's free!" I said excitedly.

The corners of her lips rose up and I knew that was a yes. I was going to leave the Dray dilemma alone until she was ready to talk about it. Pressuring her to talk when she didn't want to, only made her shut down more. I learned that early on in the past and I would let it play out on its own.

"Yes! How did you find out about that? Monty didn't mention it," she said, checking her makeup in the visor's mirror.

"I heard somebody talking about it when they were getting out of their car earlier. Now we have to figure out where the main gym is. Hit Monty up and ask him," I said, rolling my eyes.

She stopped digging in her purse and grabbed her phone to text him. We sat waiting on his reply while she reapplied her makeup and put a few eyedrops in her eyes. Her phone rang and she looked at the screen to see who it was. "What's up, bro?" she said when she answered and paused. "Okay, bet."

"What did he say?" I asked when she put the phone in her lap.

"He is on his way over here. Him and some of his boys were heading that way, so he wanted to walk with us. Plus, he got access to the front of the stage.

Kaymee knew damn well I didn't want to be bothered with Montez. This was just a way for him to watch me and try to block, but front row to watch the show was love. If I had to be nice to be up close, then that's what I would do.

"Y'all ready?" Monty asked through the window.

I jumped holding my chest because I wasn't paying attention to what was going on around us. When he said something, it scared me. Turning to address him, my words were caught in my throat and I couldn't say the slick shit that was running through my mind. Monty was looking good as hell. all I could do was nod my head and turn the key to let up the windows. I got out the truck slowly, my movements were kind of stagnant since I really hadn't been in his presence in a while other than the day I beat Mena's ass.

"How far is the gym? I'm not trying to walk if it's too far. I'd rather drive," I said without looking in his direction.

"It's not far, Poe. Actually, it's right there," he said, pointing to the building directly in front of us laughing.

I kind of felt silly trying to find a way to give him attitude, but it didn't work in my favor. The sound of his laughter tugged at my heart because I missed it so much. This was the longest we'd ever went without talking in a loving manner. Checking my feelings was a must because I wasn't falling back into the love takeover shit. I'll always love him, but the hurt overpowered anything my heart was feeling.

I noticed that Kaymee was looking around nervously. Not knowing what was on her mind had me worried a little bit. In turn, it made me start looking around, too. I knew nothing was going to jump off on the school campus, but you never could tell with the ignorant niggas of today.

"You good, bestie?" I asked her lowly.

"Yeah, you know how I am with big crowds, but I have to remember that we are on a prestigious college campus and hopefully it's safe."

"You don't have anything to worry about, sis. As long as I'm here, ain't shit shakin'. Where is your punk ass boyfriend?" he asked, addressing Mee.

She hunched her shoulders as she walked ahead of us toward the gym. The irritation was evident on her face, but unlike me, Montez wasn't going to let up easily. I didn't think Kaymee understood that we knew her better than she knew herself. Dray said something to her that wasn't right and she was being closed mouthed about it. Her head kept turning back and forth nervously. I knew she was looking for Dray to pop out any minute.

"Mee, slow down for a minute so I can holla at you," Monty said, increasing his stride to catch up with her.

Hopefully Monty would be able to get her to tell him what was up. I would hate myself if anything happened to her behind Dray's black ass. Kaymee stopped without turning around and Monty caught up to her. He grabbed her by her shoulders and peeked around to see her face. The nervousness was evident in her movements. She was wringing her fingers and I hated it.

"What's going on? I know you talked to that nigga after what you witnessed earlier. What did he have to say for himself?"

"Bro, I don't want to talk about it right now. Can we please go inside and enjoy the concert? Dray isn't what I want to focus on. What happens in the dark, always comes to light. I won't be stupid over his ass, though. I promise I will come to you if needed. I'm not worried about him and his bullshit, bro," she said, avoiding his eyes.

"Did he say or do something to you, Mee? Don't lie to me either." His nosed flared wide while he waited on her response.

"I don't want to talk about it right now, damn! Would you just leave it alone? Let's enjoy the rest of the night, please."

"Bet, you got it. I'll leave it alone for now. If I find out that nigga is doing some fuck shit to you, I'm dropping his ass on sight. You got my word on that."

Monty didn't play when it came to us and I hoped he didn't have to make good on his promise. The way he said the statement a minute ago let me know he knew about the exchange between Dray and Jonathan. He was waiting for

Dray to do something stupid and it wouldn't be good for him in the end if he acted up.

When we entered the building, Monty stopped to talk to one of the guards at the door. I didn't know what he said, but the guy handed him a couple wristbands. Monty in returned slapped hands with him and the guy immediately put something in his pocket. He walked back to Kaymee and I and handed each of us a band.

"These will get us to the front of the stage. I know how much y'all love Cardi B, so I made it happen for y'all."

He was looking at me and I knew then that he was trying to make up for his mishap. I appreciated the gesture, but this wasn't going to get him back in good with me. He would have to come better than a front row seat to a concert.

"Thank you, bro," Mee said excitedly, hugging him tightly.

"Thanks, Montez," was all I could give.

I didn't know if he was looking for more from me, but I didn't have anything else for him. The announcer introduced the *Migos* over the system and that put fire under his ass to lead the way into the auditorium. As we were led to the front, Kaymee slowed her steps and I ended up stepping on the back of her heel.

"What you stopping for, sis?" I asked, whispering in her ear. I tapped her four times on the back because I believed in superstitions.

She was looking to her right and I followed her gaze. Dray was rocking to the beat of the music, having a grand ole time with the bitch he was molesting outside. Not only was he in the wrong for the shit he was doing with the bitch, he had the nerve to still be in her presence.

"Ain't this some shit! This muthafucka foul as fuck!" I said, trying to get through the crowd to confront him.

"Poe, don't worry about it because I'm not. His ass ain't shit and I'm not dealing with it," she said, pulling me back.

Mee, don't allow his ass to disrespect you like that! You know what, if you like it, I love it."

I was pissed off because she was being nonchalant about the entire situation and I wasn't feeling it at all. Dray was going to have her out here in Atlanta looking like a damn fool. She wasn't trying to hear anything I had to say, but she was going to learn the hard way.

Catching up to Montez, we actually had seats while others were standing. Kaymee made her way to the farthest seat, leaving me to sit next to him. I wanted to ask her to switch, but I left it alone. I started rapping to "Bad and Boujee". That's what I needed to get my mind off the fact I was so close to the man I loved and hated at the same time. They sang a couple more songs and when the beat dropped for "Drip", I knew my bitch Cardi was about to pop out.

"Came through drippin'. Drip, drip. Came through drippin'. Drip, drip."

Cardi came out looking good as hell. Her body was snatched in a hot pink jumpsuit with a pair of silver Louboutin heels with pink and blond hair. She didn't look like she had given birth over a month ago. Rapping hard and hittin' a few moves, the vibe in the building was on an all time high. Everybody was turned the fuck up!

With every song she spit, the crowd was going crazy. Her fifteen minutes of fame had turned into major paper. I loved how she didn't let the bullshit deter her from coming out on top. I had to give her props. She was doing that shit and the haters were big mad.

Cardi was on stage for a good hour and Mee and I was having the time of our lives. I needed this concert to bring me out of the funk I had been in for the past month. After this, I would be able to start classes with an opened mind. The music for "Be Careful" filled the room and all the females went crazy. Many could relate to the lyrics of the song and I was one of them. I stood up out of my seat because that was my shit.

The only man, baby, I adore
I gave you everything, what's mine is yours
I want you to live your life, of course
But I hope you get what you dyin' for
Be careful with me, do you know what you're doing?
Who's feelings that you hurtin' and bruisin'
You gon' gain the whole world
But is it worth the girl that you losin'?
Be careful with me
Yeah, it's not a threat, it's a warning
Be careful with me
Yeah, my heart is like a package with a fragile label on it
Be careful with me

While I was rapping word for word with her, I could feel Monty burning a hole through the side of my face. He was the reason the song meant so much to me. I didn't regret the lack of attention I was giving him, but deep down I wanted to cozy up to him. It wasn't going to happen because I was still mad about him dipping with another bitch.

I was rocking back and forth when I peeped him moving behind me in my peripheral. Giving him the satisfaction of seeing me clock his moves by following him with my eyes was something I refused to do. It wasn't long before I felt his arms wrap around my waist.

"I miss you, Poe. I'm sorry. Please forgive me," he said lowly in my ear.

My mind was saying, nigga, please. But my lady parts were screaming, we miss you, too. It had been over a month since my kitty had been tampered with and she was ready. He didn't need to know that, so I kept rocking and he rocked along with me.

I missed him too, but the thoughts of his infidelity were still fresh in my mind. Forgiving him so easily wasn't in my plans. He had plenty of making up to do in order to get back in my good graces. His scent alone almost had me saying the complete opposite though, for real. The smell of his Versace Black cologne was tickling my nasal cavity.

Feeling my body relax in his arms, my mind replayed the words that Mena revealed. I shrugged out of his embrace and turned around to face him with an attitude. I calmed down once I saw the sadness in his eyes and that was a mistake. Before I could utter a sound, his lips were brushing against mine. Out of habit, I returned the kiss and our tongues danced to the beat of the song "Ring".

I knew the lyrics were making him think about how I had blocked him and he hadn't heard from me until today. He deepened the kiss and let Cardi express how he was feeling. Ending the kiss, he hugged me tightly and whispered, "I just miss you. I just miss us, baby," right along with the song in my ear. The tears stinging my eyes were threatening to fall. The well ran over when I felt his tears on my shoulder.

Hugging him back, I consoled him because I knew our split was hurting him just as much as it was hurting me. We would always be friends, but an item? Nah, I was good on that. When the song ended, he released me and I wiped the tears from his eyes and kissed his cheek. I stepped back when Cardi started speaking.

"Thank y'all for showing me so much love. Good night, Atlanta!" Cardi screamed into the mic before walking off stage. We cheered her on until she disappeared behind the curtain.

There were so many people trying to get out of the auditorium at once. Monty grabbed my hand leading us to the emergency exit. We made it out without having to follow the crowd. The party was far from over because someone popped their trunk and music blared through the speakers. There were women popping their ass every way my head turned. This was about to be one experience I was going to enjoy to the fullest.

Kaymee started dancing to the music and her ass was bouncing with the beat. If she didn't have nothing, she had plenty of ass. She was enjoying herself and I was glad she was smiling. A guy must've liked what he saw because he came up behind her and started dancing with her. I was cheering her on when Dray came out of nowhere and snatched her up.

"What the fuck is your problem? You must want me to beat yo' ass!" he snarled, looking down at her. She was stuck in place and didn't know what to do.

The guy stared at Dray with a look of murder on his face. "Nigga, that's not how you handle a female. Fuck wrong with you?"

"Stay the fuck outta my business, fam. You don't know what the fuck you stickin' yo' nose in. This my bitch. Don't tell me how to handle shit that belong to me! She don't know yo' ass and I don't either, so move the fuck around."

The dude hiked up his pants and swung on Dray, hitting him in the side of his head. The blow stunned him, forcing him to let Kaymee go. They started tussling and Monty came out of nowhere and punched Dray in his mouth.

"I got this nigga, homie," he said to the dude, never taking his eyes off Dray. "Didn't I tell you if you wasn't gon' do right by her to leave her the fuck alone? That's what the fuck I meant, nigga!" he said, hitting him again. "If you can't refer to her by her name, don't call her shit, period! Yo' ass was just literally in another bitch ass and you want to come grabbing on her for dancing? Get the fuck outta here with that hoe ass shit!" Monty shouted, pushing Dray in the chest.

"Monty, I'm not about to go this route with you. We better than this and you are like a brother to me. I don't tell you how to handle your girl, so don't tell me how to handle mine. Let's go, Kaymee," he said, grabbing her by the hand.

Montez snatched her by her arm and pulled her behind him. "She ain't going nowhere with you, nigga. She out here enjoying herself. If you want to leave, be my guest. She ain't going."

Dray chuckled while rubbing the top of head. He looked at Kaymee and sighed. "I don't have time for this shit. Kaymee, let's go!"

My best friend looked like a disobedient kid that was about to get a whooping as she walked toward him. Monty's chest was heaving up and down, but he didn't say shit to her. I couldn't believe she was leaving with him after he treated her like that.

"Mee—"

"Poe, I'll be right back. Don't leave me," Kaymee said calmly.

She walked away with Dray chastising her like she was a toddler. He made sure whatever he said was low, so she'd be the only one to hear the words that fell from his lips.

Chapter 3
Montez

Dray was playing with fire and I wanted to fuck him up. I left the shit alone because I couldn't make Mee see him as the good for nothing ass nigga that he was. If I would've forced her to stay, she would've found a way to get back to him anyway. That couldn't have been the first time he talked to her like that and I wasn't feeling the shit at all.

When I hit him, I put my all behind that punch, but it didn't faze his ass. In the back of my mind, a voice was telling me that something was going on with him. I just didn't know what it was. One thing I did know was he had to find somewhere else to lay his head. There was no way I would be able to live with him after this.

He had a baby on the way, numerous bitches on the side, and he was still claiming Mee as his own. Nah, not under the same roof as me he wouldn't. His life issues wouldn't do anything except bring her down. I wasn't about to stand back and let everything she worked hard for come crumbling down behind a nigga. Having a heart to heart with her was a must. Even if it meant me telling her about everything that was going on with that nigga.

I walked to my ride and grabbed the haze that I had rolled up and put fire to it. Glaring in the direction that Dray and Kaymee went, I saw them still standing there going at it with each other. I was cool as long as his bitch ass didn't put his hands on her.

"Damn, fam. What's up between you and that nigga? Y'all was tight as fuck at one point," my dude Los asked, leaning on the side of my ride. "And who is the cutie he talking to? I've never seen that one before. She bad."

“Fuck that punk! That’s my muthafuckin’ sister and I regret introducing that nigga to her,” I said, taking a pull from the blunt.

“Why would you do that dumb shit, Monty? Dray ain’t trying to be serious with no female.”

Reaching in my ride, I pulled out the bottle of Hennessy and took it to the head. In my mind, I was trying to figure out what the fuck I was thinking when I brought him into her world. Actually, I thought Kaymee would be the ideal girl to make him do right. That was before I found out about all the other shit he had going on.

“I can’t even answer that, Los. It was the wrong move to make because I’m gon’ have to fuck his ass up.”

As I leaned in my car to put the bottle back, I heard Mee scream out, “Let me go, Dray!” My head whipped in the direction they were in a minute ago, but I didn’t see them. Scanning the lot, I saw him damn near dragging her toward his car. She was struggling to get out of his grip, but he wasn’t letting go.

“What’s his fuckin’ problem?” Los asked, pushing off the car.

“I’on know, but I gave him fair warning to keep his fuckin’ hands to himself.”

Walking briskly toward them, I saw Poetry rushing to Mee’s aide. Dray paused, but still had a hold on Mee’s arm. With the way her head was moving, I knew Poe was going in on his ass. Before I knew it, Dray hauled off and slapped her, making her head swivel to the right.

Charging forward like a raging bull, I snatched my bitch off my hip. Los was right beside me as we approached his ass. There were no words spoken as I raised my tool and slapped his ass across the head with it. He automatically let Mee’s arm go and I committed to whooping his ass.

"Yo' ass don't listen, huh? Put yo' muthafuckin' hands on me, nigga!" I felt my body being snatched off of him before I shrugged out of the hold I was being held in. "Get the fuck off me!" I yelled.

"Give me the gun, Monty," Los said, grabbing my tool until he had it out of my possession. "Now, fuck that nigga up!"

Dray rose to his feet with blood running down his temple. "This what we on, Monty? I've treated you with nothing but respect and this how you repay me?"

This fool was out of his mind if he thought I was about to sit back while he put his hand on one of mine. Me and Poetry may not be together, but I'd be damned if I let her be disrespected in any way. When I rushed him, Kaymee stepped in front of him and got knocked the fuck down. There was nothing that would stop me from beating his ass. Punching his ass in his eye, I followed up with an uppercut and he staggered.

He gained his footing and came back with a clean left hook and it was on from there. A crowd gathered and we were fucking each other up. I was tired of playing with his ass. Delivering a two-piece combo to his head, his hands went up and I fucked up his ribcage. The pain he was in was noticeable because he doubled over. I hit his ass with a hard left and he fell on the ground. I lifted my foot to stomp his ass but I felt a tug on my shirt.

"Monty, that's enough! Don't do this!"

Kaymee grabbed me by my shirt, trying to pull me back. Ignoring what she said, I dropped my foot down on his head. "Muthafucka, I want yo' ass out of my shit tonight! Find one of yo' hoes to lay up wit'. I'm done with yo' ass from this point on!" I yelled as Mee pulled me back with as much force as she could. I could've broken away from her, but I was done with his bitch ass.

"You didn't have to do all that, Monty. I don't want to be the cause of y'all friendship going to shit."

"His ass is the reason our friendship is over!" I said, pointing at Dray. "You didn't have nothing to do with that. Look, I fucked that nigga up because he put his hands on Poe! If you want to keep being with that nigga, do that shit! I came over here because you were screaming for him to let you go.

If you only wanted to be saved for the moment, then you got that. You won't be able to stop me from killing his ass if I see his ass doing you wrong! If you like the bullshit he's doing, stay with his punk ass. Get ready to go through the wringer to keep him because this bullshit is just beginning!" I said, snatching away from her.

"Montez!"

She kept calling my name and I ignored her. I walked to the truck where Poetry was standing with her head down. Lifting her chin, the rage came back full force when I saw the welt on her cheek. I looked back at Dray and he was looking at me with his lip between his teeth mugging me.

"What's up, nigga? Don't stand there! Do something, bitch!" I barked at his ass.

"It's cool, Monty. Believe that shit. Kaymee, let's go," he said, walking away.

Instead of following him, she came over to the truck and opened the door to get in. "I said let's go, Kaymee!" he yelled when he realized she wasn't behind him.

"Come make her go with you, pussy!" I said, walking toward him. He laughed and walked in the direction of his car. I went around to the passenger side of the car and opened the door.

Kaymee was sitting inside the truck looking straight ahead. The sadness in her eyes tore me up. She was back at square one, in the same predicament but with a different muthafucka, in a different state. I couldn't let her get swallowed up by this nigga. I blamed myself for what was going on, but I didn't know it was like this.

"Mee, look at me," I said softly but sternly. When she turned her head toward me, a lonely tear fell from her eye. "What did he say to you?"

"Monty, I don't want to talk about it," she said, turning away from me.

"Okay, you don't want to talk, you better tell Jonathan before I do. That nigga won't be a part of my circle with his bullshit. I'm cutting his ass off and I think you should, too. I've never seen that side of him and I can't help you without killing him. I've seen niggas act that way on many occasions and the outcome wasn't good. Turning my back on you is something I would never do but, sitting back watching you suffer ain't in the plans either. Concentrate on school, sis. That nigga got too much baggage that comes along with him. Leave that shit alone."

"What do my daddy have to do with this? I'm not telling him shit and neither are you. Thank you for standing up for me. I got it from here, I promise. Poe let's go," she said without looking at me.

"He will have a lot to do with it if Dray puts his hands on you. That nigga didn't hesitate putting his hands on Poe and he don't love her! What makes you think he won't do the same to you? I'm done. If you want to let him talk to you like a child, have at it, Kaymee," I said, backing away from the truck.

Poetry got in the car and I scrambled around to the other side before she could close the door. I had to make sure she was alright. "Poe, hold up," I said, catching the door before it closed.

"What is it, Montez? I want to get Mee away from here before Dray decides he wants to come back with more bullshit."

"That nigga ain't stupid. Are you okay?" I asked, touching the bruise on her cheek.

"I'm good. I'll call you when we get to Jonathan's house. Don't call him and say shit, Montez. If you call him, just talk about business. Let Mee tell him about what's been going on with Dray on her own. I need to go lay down because my head is killing me," she said, starting the truck.

"Do you want me to drive y'all to the crib? I can have Los follow us in my whip." She sat thinking things over for a couple seconds then shook her head yeah. "A'ight, hold up. I'll be right back."

Walking over to where Los was standing talking on his phone, I dug my keys out of my pocket. As I got closer to him, I could hear him going off on whomever was on the other end of his line. Los was a cool muthafucka I met when I got down here my freshman year. I put him on and he has been by my side ever since.

When I went to Chicago, he was the one handling my business while I was gone and everything was running as if I'd never left. The nigga was as solid as they came and I fucked with him. In my mind, he was going to be the muthafucka who stood beside me making money instead of Dray's ass. I didn't even want him involved in the shit I had going on, with his snake ass.

"Aye, I gotta go. The shit you spittin' is going in one ear and out the other. There is no coming back from what you did, Chyanne. It's a wrap. I hope you find what you lookin' for in those niggas because you would never get another nigga like Carlos, baby. Be easy now and stop blowing up my line," he said, ending the call. "My bad, fam. You ready to roll?"

"I need you to drive my whip. My girl has a bad headache and I don't want her to drive. I'm gon' get them to their destination safely, then we can take care of business."

"A'ight, say less," he said as I placed my keys in his hand.

Jogging back to the truck, Kaymee had already got in the backseat and put her earbuds in her ear. That was her cue to be left alone. As I opened the driver's side door, Poe climbed over into the passenger seat and laid her head against the window closing her eyes. I sat watching her for a moment before I put the car in gear and backed out of the parking space.

The car was quiet, so I turned the radio on and adjusted the volume. It had been months since I'd been in Poe's presence and the urge to touch her was strong. Reaching over, I grabbed her hand and she squeezed mine in return. A smile formed across my lips and I let the truck lead me to Jonathan's house.

I could tell she missed me as much as I missed her, but I fucked up. I had to make things right before some other nigga tried to shoot his shot. The last four years had been good as hell between us until I got caught sticking my hand in the cookie jar.

Mena didn't mean shit to me. She was what some called "convenient pussy." In other words, she was something to do until the one I loved could grace me with her presence. Now that Poetry was older, there was no one that could take her place. I regretted cheating on her and I realized it when she basically said fuck me with her actions.

Keeping her word about not wanting to fuck with me only made me want to fight for her that much stronger. She showed me that I wasn't about to play with her heart and think it was okay. Poetry actually had a nigga ready to break down in tears asking for her forgiveness. It's been months and I wanted my girl back. It was time for me to go after what I've always wanted and that was Poetry Renee.

Chapter 4
Jonathan

The shipment from G was delivered and I needed to run some things by Monty and Dray. I needed to make sure they understood how I ran my organization was a must. The relationship between Kaymee and Dray was something I had to keep as far away from my business as possible. Killing his ass was at the top of my list, but he hasn't given me a real reason to capitalize on that shit.

When I heard his punk ass screaming at her on the phone, the thought of elimination was at the forefront of my mind. It didn't make matters any better when Kaymee defended him after the truth of Dray calling her gullible emerged. Kaymee was clueless about these niggas, especially ones that were into this street shit. It pissed me off because she was easy prey and it wouldn't take much to run game on her.

Failing her was what I felt I had done. I should've been there to school her on these muthafuckas. I meant every word I said to Dray's punk ass and was ready to show him that I didn't play when it came down to my daughter. He would've gotten away with all of that had I not been around, but I'm here now. My phone rang and it was G calling.

"What up, nephew?"

"I was calling to see how everything went with the shipment."

"Everything is copasetic. Delo and Tron had everything they were supposed to have. I'll be getting up with them tomorrow before they leave to head back to Chicago. I'm about to hit up Monty and that pussy ass nigga Dray to get their loads so they will be able to handle their business."

"You still pissed off at Dray because of Kaymee, huh? Unc, just sit back and let her deal with that on her own. Kaymee will let you know if shit ain't right. You have to let her grow up and handle her own affairs. We've all been through first time heartaches. No courtship is perfect. There will always be ups and downs. I don't think his ass is stupid enough to do anything that could cause him to eat dirt."

"He bet not do shit to hurt her. I don't give a damn what kind of mistakes I had to endure, she won't be going through any of it. She will not be out in the street feeling that she needs a man to live her life. That's exactly what Dot's ass did, look where that got her. I want more for my daughter and I will make sure she knows her worth. Speaking of Dot, what's going on with that situation?"

"I don't want any of this to come between y'all business wise. Keep your eyes open, but pay attention from afar. If he switches up, you will see it in her actions, then you start asking questions." G chuckled and I didn't know why until he continued to talk. "As far as Dot goes, she's walking around looking like a real life *Walking Dead* zombie. She's the official female Pookie, probably walking door to door, sucking dick for that rock. I was mad as fuck when you didn't let me blow her shit back. But I like what she's going through better now. I can honestly say she's dwindling nice and slow."

I felt bad for forcing her into that shit. Then again, I didn't because she left me and my daughter for dead when she pulled the trigger to end our lives. The scars that I would wear for the rest of my life reminds me everyday of the bullshit she pulled. Fuck Dot with her funky ass.

"I got a nigga that wants to buy four of them joints. So that's fifty off top. I'm sending that back to you."

"That's good shit! Send twenty and keep twenty-five for yourself. Give the rest to Kaymee. She deserves that shit. That nigga would never be able to say what the fuck he did for her."

"You already know as long as I have breath in my body, she's good. Even if I died, she still wouldn't need shit from his ass. She will forever be straight because I have shit lined up for her."

"Bae, I need you to get something off the top shelf in the bedroom. I can't reach it!" Katrina yelled like she was out of her damn mind.

"Nephew, I gotta go. The lady needs me right now. I'll holla at you later."

"A'ight, remember what I said about cuz. She gon' be good. Keep a level head, unc," he said, hanging up.

I walked up the stairs slowly with my baby girl on my mind. She was blossoming into a woman and I knew I would have to let her handle that nigga. I was still going to be there to fuck his ass up when he got out of his body.

Entering our bedroom, I went straight to the closet and Katrina wasn't there. I heard her rustling around in the bathroom and headed in that direction. When I stepped through the door, my mouth dropped to the floor. The sight before me was breathtaking.

My baby stood before me in black, laced panties with the matching bra, as well as black garters that held up a pair of sheer pantyhose with a crotchless center. Topping the entire getup off with a pair of sexy stilettos that had her legs looking like they belonged on a stallion. Her hair was bone straight with a part down the middle and it framed her face perfectly. The smoky eye makeup made her appear devious as hell. The red lipstick she wore was going to look scrumptious wrapped around my joint.

I had a bad bitch in Katrina. She eased her ass on the sink sexily and gapped her legs opened. Her kitty gleamed in the lighting and it was a beautiful sight. Rubbing her bud slowly, her manicured fingers was caressing it seductively. When they disappeared inside her tunnel, I rocked up instantly.

"Daddy, I need help putting out this fire that's burning between my legs," she whispered lowly as she brought the very fingers that she had in her snatch to her luscious lips.

No longer able to contain myself, I pushed off the door jam and walked toward her. Running my thumb up and down her slit, she let out a soft moan. Katrina had teased me to the point I was speechless. Now I had to respond with action and I hoped she was ready.

Staring in her eyes, I moved my fingers in a circular motion along her clit. Her eyes lowered with every movement. "Open yo' muthafuckin' eyes. I want to see every emotion when you nut on my fingers, Trina."

Her breathing quickened and I knew she was about to explode. Inserting two of my fingers into her love box, I continued to massage her clit with my thumb. She was gripping the edge of the counter as best she could. Every stroke of my finger hit her G-spot each time. The grip she had on it excited me because I knew she was right where I needed her to be. Curling my finger repeatedly in the 'come here' gesture, she leaned back and squirted all over the front of my pants and shirt.

"Aaaaaaah, yesssssss!" she screamed out.

I wasn't about to let her come down from the sexual high I had her on. As I snatched my shirt off, I dropped to my knees and lifted her legs up, burying my face in her center. She was trying to get away from the assault I was putting on her twat, but I wasn't having that. This was what she wanted when she screamed for me to come help her get something from the shelf.

Pulling her into my mouth, I clamped down on her bud and suckled softly. "Shit, Jonathan! Sssssss," she moaned as she grabbed the back of my head.

My nose was pressed against her fat pussy and I had to pause to take in a few breaths from my mouth. Her juices tasted like mango and that was my favorite fruit. Sticking my tongue into her wetness, I scooped up as much as possible before making my way lower to her ass.

I pulled her completely off the counter and threw her legs in the air. When my tongue covered her asshole, I felt her legs relax in the crevices of my arm. I don't care how many niggas say they won't put their mouth on their woman's ass, they lying.

"Ooooooouuuu, shit! Yessss, baby," she moaned as she rocked her hips faster into my mouth.

Reaching between her legs, she stroked her lower lips fast and I knew she was on the brink of coming again. I lapped at her ass and she squirted in the air and it rained all over me. I didn't give a fuck because my woman was overly satisfied.

I let her legs down and stood up. Snatching my sweat-pants down to my feet, I stepped out of them and kicked them behind me. As I rubbed my pipe along her wet pussy, I decided not to take her in that position. I grabbed her arms and lowered her to the floor and pushed her against the wall. Murdering her kitty was the only thing on my mind.

With my hand holding the back of her neck, I bent my knees and guided myself inside her hot oven. "Mmmmm, this muthafucka tight as fuck, Trina," I said, moving in and out of her wetness. Gripping her waist, I fucked her long and hard against the wall.

I was a second away from spilling all my babies inside of her. It wasn't time because I was just getting started. Biting down on her shoulder, I hit her with a couple long strokes before I had to pull out and back away from the pussy. Tapping my dick against her mound to send my seeds back to my nut sack, she turned around and wrapped her arms around my neck.

Taking that opportunity to lift her off her feet, I positioned her on the wall and graced her with all nine inches of my manhood. "Oooohhhhhh, yeah! Fuck me, baby!" she said as her nails dug in my shoulders. "Right there! Don't stop! I'm cummin'!"

"I'm there with you, baby. Let that shit go!" I grunted, trying to hold off until she got hers.

The walls of her love box tightened around my pipe and I lost all control and bust at the same time she did. Her nectar cascaded onto the floor, splashing my feet and my legs. "Fuck, Trina! Wooooooo, shit!"

She was milking my nuts for all I had. She was throwing her ass back and I was ready to collapse where I stood. When my dick slipped out, I fell against the sink using my hands to hold on so I wouldn't fall.

Katrina still had her face against the wall. The shit was humorous because she looked like she had fallen asleep where she stood. That session was a good one and all I wanted to do was shower and get my black ass in the bed.

Leaning over to start the shower, I let the water run before I started taking her lingerie off so we could wash all the sex remnants from our bodies. Round two would be in full effect before we got out. I was ready to give my baby money to go to the salon bright and early in the morning because she was about to fuck that hairdo up.

Chapter 5
Kaymee

The night of the block party, Dray called my phone nonstop for the rest of the night. I didn't answer because I wanted him to see what it felt like to be ignored. The threats he threw at me scared me at first, but I was over that shit. Dray was probably crazy, but he wasn't that damn crazy to try anything. I believed he was just trying to control me. Dot did enough of that my entire life so he could go ahead with all that.

After Montez drove us back to my dad's house, he and Poetry sat talking for a little while before she came inside and went to sleep. She had been complaining about headaches before we left Chicago, so maybe it was stress. Poetry and Monty had been going through so much in the past couple months. It was messing with her more than she was putting on, but she would never admit it.

We were on campus to pick up our keys to the dorm. I also wanted to talk to my advisor to see if I was on the right track with my classes. We walked to the advisory office and it wasn't too crowded when we arrived. After signing in, we sat in the chairs that were set up in the lobby to wait for our names to be called.

"I'm excited about moving into the dorm. Being on my own is something I'm ready for," Poetry said, reaching in her purse. She pulled out a pack of Now and Laters. Her stingy ass opened one up and started smacking on it like it was a steak dinner without offering me any.

"You ain't gon' offer a bitch a piece?" I asked nastily.

"Damn, Mee. You know I hate sharing my damn candy! Here, don't ask for no mo' because it ain't none," she said, shoving a piece into my hand. "Have you heard from Dray?

“Yeah, I heard from him but I haven’t responded to him at all. What he’s on is not what I want. Until he can show me that I mean something to him, I’m good on that.”

“All I will say is this. Don’t let him put you in a funk. You are beautiful and when man was made, it didn’t stop at his good for nothing ass.”

“Kaymee Morrison.”

Before I could respond, my name was called to go to the office of my advisor. “I’ll be right back. I hope they call you soon so we can get out of here,” I said, grabbing my purse and standing up.

Walking in the direction of the woman that called my name, another woman came out and called Poetry’s name. We walked down the hall and went into the offices of our appointed advisors. I sat down in front of the desk and glanced at the nameplate that read, *Lorinda Parker*. She looked to be about my age but I couldn’t tell because black don’t crack.

“Hello, Kaymee. My name is Mrs. Parker. I will be your advisor for your entire education experience here at Spelman. I took the liberty of going over your transcripts last night by request of the Dean. She was very impressed with your academics and personally placed your education in my hands. For her to do such a thing, you have come to us full of greatness,” she said, smiling brightly.

Mrs. Parker was telling me these things as if I didn’t know what was in my file. I fought hard to keep my grades up so I would excel when I went off to college. Failing in school was something I didn’t have any intentions of doing all my life.

“I have a question for you. Were you ever approached in school about skipping ahead?”

As I sat thinking about how much to reveal for a few seconds, I decided to tell the truth. "Yes, it was mentioned many times actually. Unfortunately, my mother didn't think I was smart enough to skip to a higher grade. Each time it was brought to her attention, she declined."

"Kaymee, didn't your mom see the grades that you were bringing home every semester?"

"Of course she saw them, Mrs. Parker. Did she give a damn what was printed in black and white? No. But I don't want to talk about my mother. I am a very independent young woman that will continue to strive in this world on her own without the help of her mother. Where are you going with this conversation?" I asked.

Trying not to be a bitch about the situation, I pushed the anger that tried to creep inside of me to the side. I sat staring her in the eyes, waiting on her to continue. As she shuffled through the papers on her desk, I waited patiently for her to start talking again.

"What I'm about to tell you may come as a shock to you, but I want you to know that I will be here to witness everything you are going to accomplish here at Spelman. You have received a scholarship which will pay your tuition through graduation. That's just the tip of the iceberg though, Kaymee. You have enough credits under your belt to enter this school year as a Junior. What that means is —"

"I am a third-year student of Spelman University at the age of eighteen. That's not a surprise to me. I pushed myself to be the best that I could be since the age of six. I've had plans to be somebody from the moment I learned to read. The credits that I have towards my nursing degree is what I want to hear about. I'm sorry if I'm appearing rude, it's not intentional. I'm just trying to find out where do I go from here."

Mrs. Parker sat and smiled at me like a proud parent. "Miss Morrison, you will have to do two years of nursing, starting on Wednesday. I have your classes here in front of me and I believe you will excel in whatever you set out to do," she said, sliding a few pieces of paper toward me. "Here is the map of the campus as well as your class schedule. If there is anything you may need, don't hesitate emailing me," she said, handing me her business card. "My business and direct number is on there, as well.

You will go to the bookstore to retrieve your books and any supplies you may need. It is included in your scholarship. You will receive a laptop computer as well as a printer for your studies. For now, we will go to the other side of the building so you can take a photo and receive your campus identification badge. Lastly, I'll direct you in the right direction to pick up the keys to your dorm. Welcome to Spelman, Kaymee. Make me proud," she said with a smile.

"Thank you so much," I said, standing up with my hand outstretched.

"You're more than welcome. Let's go so you can get settled into this place of greatness."

***

As I was getting the keys to the dorm, my phone buzzed. I looked down to see who was calling and it was Dray. Declining the call, I grabbed the keys that were handed to me. "Thank you. Would it be possible to get the other key, please? My best friend is my roommate and I can actually give it to her."

"No, she will have to come down to get the key herself. I'm sorry."

My phone vibrated again and I rolled my eyes thinking it was Dray again. Looking down I noticed it was Poetry and I hurried to answer. "It's okay. She will come down when she's finished talking to her advisor. Thank you, again," I said, turning away from her.

"Hey, Poe. Are you finished?"

"Yeah, I'm on my way to get the keys to the dorm. Where you at?"

"I'm already here. I'll sit and wait for you because you have to pick your key up yourself. Hurry up."

"Okay, I'll be there in five minutes," she said, hanging up.

I sat in an empty chair, scrolling through social media when I overheard two females talking. There was a lot of messiness going on as usual, so I read and kept on scrolling. I didn't have time for the bullshit that people were involved in, but it was comical though. The voice of one of the females became louder and my interest peaked.

"Dray better stop playing with me. He knows how I feel about him, but since we spent time together and that bitch blew up his spot, he's been acting real funny."

"Alexis, what did you expect? Dray hasn't given you any indication that what y'all got going on was gonna be anything other than fuckin'. You set yourself up if you believed otherwise."

When I heard Dray's name, I tried hard not to look around to see who was talking. The name Alexis let me know it was the girl from the block party. As I continued to scroll through my timeline, the feeling of being watched was strong.

"Come on, Lexi. This is not what we are here for. Let's get the key and leave," her friend said lowly.

"Fuck that! I need to know what role she plays in his life since he ain't talking."

Glancing up from my phone, I looked at what's her name like she was a damn fool. I knew that she let the pretty face fool her ass because she was storming over like a pit bull ready to attack. The funny thing about it, I wasn't worried.

"Can I talk to you for a minute?" Alexis had the nerve to ask.

"Sure, as long as you ain't on bullshit. What is it that you want to talk about? Don't say Drayton either because whatever y'all got going on is just that, what *y'all* got going on."

"I want to know what's your relationship with him. I have been dealing with him for two years and if you are claiming him as your man, I need to know."

Chuckling, I held my head down. "That's where you went wrong," I said, looking up at her. "If you have to question the next bitch about what's going on with *your man,* there's no way he is solely yours. The muthafucka you need to be questioning is his ass, not me. What I have going on with Dray is something of the past since I saw him molesting your ass in public. Anything else?" I asked nicely.

"Yeah, where did you meet him?"

"That's none of your business. Now you're prying into my life. Move around, baby girl, because I'm not the one that owes you an explanation. I advise you to go question his hoe ass and get the fuck away from me."

"What she said. You hoes don't want no smoke this way. My girl said move the fuck around, so that's what you better do because ain't shit but space and opportunity in this bitch," Poetry said, walking up behind them.

The look on Alexis' face said she was about to say some slick shit out of her mouth. Her girl must've sensed it as well because she pulled her by the arm. "Come on Lexi, let's go."

"This ain't over, you will tell me what the fuck I want to know sooner than later," Alexis said walking backwards.

"Was that a threat? The last bitch that got out of her body probably don't remember the shit that happened to her. I'm not worried though. When you come at me again, make sure you not selling wolf tickets," I said as I winked at her.

Once they walked away, I could still hear Alexis talking shit. It didn't faze me by far. Whoever came to me with bullshit was going to get the treatment I never gave my mama for years. There was a lot of pent up frustration that I was ready to unleash.

"What the hell was that about?" Poetry asked.

"Dray's ass. Go get that key so we can get out of here. I'm hungry as hell."

"Fuck Dray!" Poetry said, walking to the desk.

I laughed out loud because she was too serious about how she felt about him. She loved him the entire time in Chicago and was team Dray. Now she wanted his ass far, far, away. Watching Poetry walk away, I noticed that she was off balance a little bit. She reached the desk and it seemed like she was holding on for dear life. I jumped up and raced to her side.

"You good, sis?" I asked.

She shook her head yes, but the expression on her face said another story. Poetry gave the woman behind the desk her identification as I held her around her waist. The way she was swaying had me worried.

"Are you okay, baby?" the woman asked, giving her the keys and her identification back. "You don't look too good."

"I'm okay, thanks," Poetry said as she placed the items in her purse. "Let's go. I think I need to eat something," she said, turning around.

It was a good thing I was holding on to her because as soon as I started walking behind her, she passed out in my arms. “Call an ambulance! Poetry wake up!” I screamed. The woman behind the desk was on the phone while other people came over to help me.

“What happened?” one guy asked as he checked for a pulse.

“I don’t know. She just fainted. She said she was okay when I asked a few minutes ago.”

“The ambulance is on the way. Keep trying to get her to wake up,” the woman at the desk yelled. “They want to know if she has any known medical conditions and if she may be pregnant.”

“No, she doesn’t and she’s definitely not pregnant,” I responded.

Someone brought a cold paper towel over and handed it to me. I wiped it over her face, but Poetry still didn’t budge. I wasn’t too worried because her chest was moving so I knew she was breathing. All I wanted was for her to wake up and say something.

“Move aside, please!” the paramedic shouted. “How old is she?” he asked.

“She’s eighteen,” I answered without looking up.

He laid her down flat on the floor and lifted her eyelids with his thumb before he shined a light into her eyes. His partner placed an oxygen mask over her nose and mouth before they slid a board underneath her and placed her on the stretcher. I could see her eyes fluttering and she was struggling to open them.

“She’s coming around. We have to get her to the hospital to see what’s going on,” the female paramedic stated.

“I’m coming with her, if that’s alright.”

"Yes, that's fine," she said as they wheeled her toward the door.

Grabbing my purse as well as Poe's, I damn near ran out the door watching them load her into the ambulance. The male paramedic helped me into the ambulance as the female ran to the driver's seat. Once he was inside, he yelled for her to go while beating on the side of the ambulance.

"What hospital are you taking her to?" I asked in a shaky voice as I pulled my phone out of my purse.

"We are going to Grady's on Decatur Street Southeast," he said as he wrapped the blood pressure cuff on her arm.

Finding Monty's number, I pressed the button and waited for him to answer. "What's up, Mee?"

"Bro, get to Grady's hospital. Poetry passed out and we are in the ambulance on our way there. I don't know what happened, just meet me there."

"Okay. You good?" he asked.

"No, I'm not. I won't be until I know she's gonna be alright," I said, watching the paramedic take multiple tubes of blood.

"I'm getting in the car now. I'll be there shortly. Everything will be okay," he said before hanging up.

Poetry was trying to take the oxygen mask off as we pulled up to the emergency room entrance. The paramedic was fighting with her to keep it on. That gave me hope she would be fine. I patted her on her leg so she would know that I was there.

"Poe, keep the mask on. You fainted and you need the oxygen right now," I explained.

She stopped fighting and I saw a tear fall from her eye into her ear. The back door opened and the female paramedic held her hand out to help me get down. They took her out of the ambulance and rushed her into the hospital. I followed closely behind with my nerves going wild.

Chapter 6
Drayton

Trying to get in contact with Kaymee had become a chore for me. It also made me madder than a muthafucka. I didn't know why she insisted on being on my bad side. Threatening her didn't seem to work. I guess she thought I was playing with her ass or something. Playtime was over, though. She was about to learn to stop playing with me.

I was at Jonathan's empire because he called me and Monty to come through. There were two of G's guys there and Los was there, as well. I didn't even know he was part of the squad. I knew he worked with Monty on the street, but why he was the only one there was the question I had in my mind.

"What's up y'all? I asked y'all to come through so I could run some shit down to ya," Jonathan said once he finished his phone call. "Delo and Tron delivered the goods and each of you will be leaving here with your loads. I don't know how the two of you work, but if G says y'all got this shit, I stand by what he says."

"About that, fam. I think we need to change shit up a little bit," Monty said, cutting Jonathan off.

I knew his ass was still in his feelings about what happened at the block party. If anybody should've had a problem, it should be me. Letting that shit get in the way of my money was something I wasn't going to feed into.

"Talk to me, Montez. What do you suggest?" Jonathan asked.

Monty shot daggers in my direction and if looks could kill, I'd be a dead nigga. "I want to get the hard shit and let Dray hold on to the pills. I got my mans Los right here that's gon' help me move the dope and keys."

"Nigga, what? You out yo' muthafuckin' mind! I won't be pushed to the side just because you mad, nigga. We stickin' to the plan that was in place before we got back down here. Ain't no change of fuckin' plans!"

"Nigga—"

"Hold the fuck up! What's the problem with y'all?" Jonathan asked, looking back and forth between the two of us. He grilled my ass, but his demeanor softened when he looked at Monty. "Somebody better get to talking because this right here is something we ain't about to do. Now tell me what's up."

"Do you want to tell him what's up, Dray or should I?" Monty snarled at me.

I took a deep breath and looked at Jonathan. I wasn't about to lie to the nigga, but I wasn't telling him the whole truth either. I wasn't stupid. He could take the shit for whatever he thought it was.

"Kaymee and I had a disagreement the other day. In turn, Monty and I got into an altercation about it. Now I guess he don't want to work with me. He even put me out the crib we shared, but it's cool."

"That's all? This some bullshit on both parts. If little shit like that got y'all going at each other's heads, ain't no telling what else could interfere with shit moving around here. Chalk that shit up and let's move on," Jonathan said.

"Hell naw, that ain't it! Nigga you gon' give half the muthafuckin' story?" Monty said, laughing. "That's some bitch ass shit, Dray. Tell the whole muthafuckin' story like the Billy badass you portrayed yourself to be the other day, nigga! You know what? don't worry about it!" Monty yelled at me. "I'm not working with this nigga. Me and Los got this shit. Fuck him!"

"You know what? Don't worry about it, Jonathan. Give me the pills. I'll get 'em off like tic tacs. I don't have a problem with it. You got what you wanted fam, we good."

I had to agree with what he said before he blurted out the shit I did and Jonathan killed my ass. Getting back with Kaymee was my focus and if I had to push pills to do it, that's what I would do. Monty better stay in his lane though. Forgetting we used to be tight wouldn't be hard if he came at me again.

"Okay, it's settled then. Montez get that black duffle bag on the table. Dray, the blue one is all yours. Y'all know how to reach me if need be, don't hesitate to hit me up. I want y'all to squash whatever beef there is between the two of y'all. Don't bring that shit into my establishment. We are one, I don't give a fuck how we feel about the next mutha-fucka. Is that understood?" Jonathan asked.

Monty's phone rang and he answered it. He talked for a few minutes and hung up. "Aye, Jonathan. I gotta roll out. But I hear ya, fam," he said as Jonathan's phone rang.

"Hold on a minute," he said to Monty. "Hello. Is she alright? Okay, I'll be there in a few. Love you, baby. Think positively. She is going to be fine," he said, hanging up the phone. "I guess you got the call too, huh? We may as well head that way together. Dray, Kaymee may need you right now. Let's go."

"She don't' want to see that nigga," Monty said, snatch-ing the bag off the table and heading for the door. Los looked at me and followed him out.

"What's going on? Is Kaymee hurt?" I asked Jonathan as I grabbed the bag off the table.

"Nah, something happened to Poetry. Delo and Tron, thank y'all for your services. Let me know when y'all touch down in the Chi," he said, shaking up with them before we left out the building.

"What hospital are they at?" I asked as I popped the trunk of my ride. Stashing the bag in the secret compartment, I slammed it shut.

"Grady's on Decatur Street Southeast. I'll see you there," Jonathan said as he locked up.

I jumped in my ride, eager to get to the hospital to see Kaymee. It didn't take too long to get there. Pulling into the parking lot, I saw Monty's car and parked a ways from him. As I walked to the entrance, my phone vibrated and Alexis' name popped up on the screen. Seeing her name made my joint swell up. She had that grade A head, but she was looking for more than I was willing to give.

Declining her call as I continued into the hospital, I'd call her back later. Looking around the waiting room, I saw Kaymee and Monty sitting side by side. Jonathan was standing across the room against the wall on the phone. He must've taken a shortcut or something because he got there fast. I took a seat where Kaymee could see me and she rolled her eyes as she kept talking to Monty. It was cool. I would get a chance to rap with her.

Los was sitting in a seat watching baseball on the TV. I noticed that he would glance at Kaymee every now and again, which pissed me off. If he thought he had a chance to snatch my bitch, he had another thing coming. That was all me and somebody better let him know what it was before he got fucked up.

"Why is he here?" I heard Kaymee try to whisper.

"I came to check on my girl. That's why I'm here," I said, staring at her.

"Alexis ain't here, nigga. You can leave if you think I needed you here with me. I'm good," she said, rolling her eyes.

"Calm that shit down, Mee. Don't cause a scene. Ignore that shit, sis," Monty said.

"We need to talk, Kaymee. Can you at least hear me out?"

"There's nothing to talk about. You said what you had to say the other day. I'm cool on you."

"Do you remember what I said, though?" I asked evilly. Her whole demeanor changed when I challenged her. I didn't care who was in the room, she was going to talk to me if she wanted to or not. It wasn't up for discussion.

"I don't know what you said, bitch ass nigga. Let me in on that shit!" Monty said, turning to face me.

"This ain't got shit to do with you. Kaymee, let me holla at you," I said, standing up.

She pushed herself up out the chair and Monty grabbed her hand. Looking down at him, Kaymee patted him on his hand to release her. That's what the fuck I thought. She didn't want me to show my ass in that muthafucka.

"Where you going, baby?" Jonathan asked as he pulled his phone away from his ear.

"I'm going outside to talk to Drayton. I'll be back," she said, walking to the door.

When we got outside, she stood by the door. I grabbed her by the arm and walked her around the corner. Slamming her against the wall, I got in her face. The shocked expression she wore on her face let me know she was scared.

"Yo' ass gon' stop getting jazzy at the lip when you're talking to me. When I tell yo' ass something, you better listen!" She looked down at her feet and I snatched her head up by her chin. "I meant what the fuck I said when I told you ain't no breaking up. Kaymee don't think you gon' hide behind Monty and yo' daddy. I'm the muthafucka that you answer to. That shit with Alexis ain't shit."

"If it ain't nothing, why did she approach me trying to find out what kind of relationship I had with *her man*? You will not have your cake and eat it too, Dray. I would rather be by my damn self before I subject myself to your bullshit. I'm letting you know right now, I will not be your human punching bag.

Your threats are not moving me. I've had enough abuse from my mama. Trying to scare me back into your life is something I will not tolerate. If you are gonna beat my ass, do that shit. I guarantee you won't live to talk about it."

The fear that rested in her eyes a moment ago was gone. I had to fix this shit because I didn't want her to hate me. To hear her say that Alexis questioned her pissed me off because that bitch didn't have any right to approach her. Plus, if I'm not mistaken, I told her stupid ass to stay away from Kaymee.

"Look, I'm sorry for the way I handled you. I don't want to end things between us, Kaymee. The love I have for you is real, baby. Do you accept my apology?"

"No, I don't accept your apology because this is the second time you threatened to hurt me. The real you is coming out and I don't like this new Drayton Montgomery. Or is this who you really are? Maybe I got introduced to the decoy and got fluked. Whatever the case, I'm not into sharing and you got too much baggage for me."

My blood was boiling on the inside because I just told her stupid ass that I wasn't willing to let her go. But she kept talking about what she won't deal with. Calming down, I told her what she wanted to hear.

"Kaymee, I would never hurt you. Hearing you say it was over between us upset me. I've apologized for what you walked up on at the block party—"

"Dray, you didn't apologize once about that! Come on now, save that shit. Be honest with me. Why are you trying so hard to hold on to me? Please don't say because you love me either. If you loved me, you would have never disrespected me, even if you weren't expecting me to see the shit you were doing," she said, cutting me off.

"You right, Kaymee. I was dead wrong for dancing like that with Alexis. I thought I apologized to you. I'm sorry. Do you accept my apology?"

"Is that what you called what you were doing to her?" she asked, laughing. "That shit was borderline fuckin'! Look, all I'm asking is for you to give me time. I can't forgive you right now and I don't know when I would be able to do so. You or your hoes will not disrespect me. Get yourself together first, then come back and show me that I'm all you need.

Until then, I will concentrate on school. I don't need this, whatever you call it, distracting me from what I came to Atlanta to accomplish. I'm going back in to check on my best friend. You can leave because I don't want you here," she said, walking back to the emergency entrance.

"Kaymee!" I yelled at her back. She stopped and looked over her shoulder at me. "I love you." My heart dropped when she didn't acknowledge that shit and continued to walk away.

***

I got in my car without a destination in mind. As I rode down the street, my phone rang. A number I didn't recognize popped up on the screen. I pressed the button on the steering wheel and answered the call.

"Hello," I spoke out loud in the car.

"Yes, may I speak with Drayton Montgomery, please?"

"Speaking. Who is this?"

"This is Sheila from Bradley Realty. I'm calling about the apartment you inquired about on our website. I was wondering if you were available to come and take a tour today."

"Yes, I can be on my way now. Would you be kind enough to send the address to me via text? I can be there within the hour."

"Sure, I can do that and I look forward to seeing you, Mr. Montgomery," Sheila said, ending the call.

She sent the text and I glanced at the message and knew exactly where I was going. I loved the virtual pictures I saw online and it was the place I wanted. I hoped it looked like the pictures. I was giving the money to her before I left if it did.

It took me thirty minutes to get to the location. I dialed the number that Sheila called me from and she answered, letting me know she was waiting in the lobby for me. Parking my car, I got out and went into the building. There was a lounge area with furniture that looked comfortable as hell in the lobby. They had a computer room to the left of the lounge area.

I saw a woman sitting on the sofa and I walked over to her assuming she was Sheila. "Sheila?" I asked uncertainly.

"Yes, you must be Drayton. Nice to meet you. The unit that we have available is on the second floor. Let's head on up and, hopefully, you like it. I will first show you everything that's available in the building. You may have seen the computer lounge that we provide. It's open until ten pm.

Down this hall is the fitness center that is available to all residents. It's twenty-four hours, so you can come down to workout whenever you feel the need. There's an indoor pool that's available until ten pm, as well."

I was in awe with all the amenities the building provided. No wonder the rent was so high, but I was ready to pay for it. Sheila led the way to the elevator and pressed the button.

"What do you think so far?" she asked.

"I like everything I've seen. I won't be able to give an honest response until I see the spot that matters, the apartment."

"Absolutely," she said and chuckled. "I see you are a student at Morehouse College," she said, glancing at the application in her hand.

"Yes, I'm a Junior. Majoring in engineering."

"That's great! We give student discounts, but we will talk about that once you decide if you're moving in or not."

"Sounds good to me," I said as the doors to the elevator opened. I stepped on after Sheila and she pressed the button for the second floor. The apartment was at the end of the hall when we stepped off the elevator. There was a huge window that overlooked a park and it was beautiful. I only imagined what the view was like from the apartment.

Sheila unlocked the door and the first thing I noticed were the hardwood floors. It reminded me of my parents' house and I loved them. I closed the door and walked deeper inside following a long hall. There was a bathroom on the right a short distance from the front door, the kitchen was opened up to the living room, and the bedroom was down a short hall. Walking into the room, I was sold when I saw it had a balcony and a bathroom. The rooms were pretty spacious.

"I'll take it," I said as I checked out the closet."

“Like I was saying downstairs, we give students a discount. So, instead of twelve hundred a month, your rent will be nine hundred dollars until you graduate from school. After that, if you decide to stay, the rent will increase to the original price. Today you will need eighteen hundred dollars to close the deal. That’s first month’s rent and security.”

I removed my checkbook from my back pocket and used the wall to write out the check. After signing it, I handed the check to Sheila and she led the way back into the kitchen because I had paperwork to complete. Within the hour, I had a place to call my own.

I left out with Sheila and jumped in my whip to go get my shit out of Monty’s crib. *Fuck that nigga, I didn’t need him,* I said to myself as I drove off.

Chapter 7
Poetry

I'd been sitting in this hospital for hours and I was ready to leave. They wanted to run all types of test and there was no need for all of that. The reason I fainted was because I hadn't eaten. All I needed to do was pick up something on the way to Jonathan's house and lay my ass down.

"Poetry, we have you scheduled for a CT scan and an MRI," the nurse said as she looked at my chart.

"That won't be necessary. All I need is something to eat. I will be fine."

"We want to make sure that's all it is. It's important to check everything to ensure you are healthy and there are no major concerns we should know about."

I was getting really irritated by the nurse trying to keep me in this hospital. The only thing I'd been doing was sitting in the room waiting. I could be in my dorm doing the same thing without being charged a dime. Jonathan helped us move in the other day and I loved the privacy that came with living with only my best friend.

"I'm telling you, I don't want any test! There's nothing wrong with me! I'm ready to get out of here. This IV has my hand swollen and it's turning purple!" I said, rubbing the top of my hand.

"I'll check it for you," the nurse said, placing my chart on the counter and reached for a pair of gloves. Examining my hand, she took the IV out. Blood slowly ran out and she caught it with a cotton ball. "This wasn't inserted correctly and I apologize for that. I'll have to reinsert it."

Pulling my hand back, I looked at her like she was crazy. "Naw, I'm good on that. Would you get my discharge papers together, please? I will not continue to sit around waiting for you to run test after test just to tell me everything's normal. The ambulance ride alone is going to cost me a thousand dollars!" I exclaimed.

"Poetry, I understand your concern, but you have to allow us to do our job."

"I am, on somebody else! Do I look like a lab rat to you? Y'all won't be experimenting on me! Fuck it, I'll sign myself out of this bitch," I said, getting out of the bed.

The nurse saw that I was serious. She grabbed my chart and walked out without uttering another word. I wasn't about to play with these doctors. There was nothing wrong with me. After dressing, I sat back on the bed and waited. They had fifteen minutes to come back before I got up and walked out.

There was a soft knock on the door and then it opened. Kaymee came in with a worried expression on her face. "Poetry, why are you dressed? The nurse said you are refusing to take the tests they scheduled for you."

"Kaymee, I don't need any tests. I'm fine. I haven't eaten. That's all it is," I said irritably.

The door opened again and in walked Monty. Shooting an evil glare at Kaymee, she held her head down to avoid looking at me. She knew I was pissed because the only way Monty was there was if she called him. When Jonathan walked in the room, I was floored but, the anger went out the window.

"Poetry, why are you trying to leave without letting these doctors make sure you're good?" Jonathan asked as he closed the door. "I told your parents that I would look after you while you're here in Atlanta. I need you to take all the tests they're offering."

"Jonathan, I can't afford the bills that—"

"You don't have to pay for shit as long as I'm around. I gave you a whole car. Don't you think I would pay your medical bills just the same? Your health is important to me and I will treat you the same as my own daughter. We will be here until they say everything is alright with you," he said, gathering me in his arms.

"Thank you, Jonathan. I really don't think it's necessary to go through with the tests, though. I feel a lot better than I did a couple hours ago. I'm a little weak because I'm hungry, but other than that, I'm fine."

"Poe, would you do it for me?" Monty asked lowly.

I looked up at him and he looked worried. With everything that we've been through, I couldn't deny the fact that this man loved my dirty draws. There was never a time he hadn't been there for me. Even when he was tricking off, Monty dropped everything to make sure I was okay.

"I will stay, but it won't be for you," I said as there was a knock on the door.

The doctor walked in with papers in his hands. Looking around the room, he smiled letting the door close behind him. "Hello, everyone. My name is Dr. McCoy and I have been looking after Miss Parker. It's good to see that her family is here with her. Is it appropriate for me to discuss your results in their presence?" he asked.

"Sure, I don't have anything to hid," I said confidently. "And what results are you speaking of?"

"Your blood was taken on the ride here and we ran tests on it. Well Poetry, I think I know the cause of your fainting spell. Can you recall the last time you had a menstrual cycle?" Instead of thinking about the last time I used a tampon, my mind was too busy trying to figure out why he was asking such a question.

"Poetry, did you hear what he asked?" Monty asked.

"Um, I had one last month. Or maybe it was the month before. Shit, I didn't have one last month, I don't think. I really can't remember to be honest," I said nervously. "What does this have to do with anything, Dr. McCoy?"

"Well your bloodwork came back and the pregnancy test came back positive," he said in a cheerful voice. "You're pregnant."

"Pregnant! I haven't had sex in months. There's no way I can be pregnant," I screamed, looking at Monty. His ass was smiling hard as fuck, but I wasn't sharing his enthusiasm at all.

"According to the tests, yes, you're pregnant. I want to conduct an ultrasound to see how far along you are. Congratulations and I'll be back shortly," he said, leaving out the room.

When Dr. McCoy left out of the room, it was so quiet, you could hear a pin drop. Kaymee was sitting with her mouth hung open, Jonathan had a look of disappointment on his face, and Monty was still smiling like a proud papa. Me, I was ready to find the first damn bridge to jump off of. I'd been fucking around with Monty for years and we have never had a pregnancy scare. Now all of a sudden, there was a whole baby growing inside of me.

My parent's reaction was the first thing that came to mind. How the hell was I supposed to tell them that I was in college and pregnant? They were going to be so disappointed in me. I had done everything correctly up until this point. Now I had messed up by getting pregnant.

"Kaymee, Jonathan, would y'all give us a minute, please?" Monty asked.

Both of them looked over at me and I nodded my head. I knew Kaymee wasn't going to leave until I said it was okay to do so. When the door closed behind them, the tears fell from my eyes. I didn't know what I was going to do with a baby. Dropping out of school was something I wasn't ready to do. I'd come too far to fuck up my education to raise a baby.

"Talk to me, Poe," Monty said, reaching for my hands.

"I can't have this baby, Monty. I got through four years of high school and made it to college. There's no way I can go to school and raise a baby. Abortion is the only way to go," I cried.

"Poe, abortion is not an option. We laid down and made a baby and we will stand up and take care of it. I know things have been pretty fucked up between us, but I will never turn my back on you. I messed up, I've admitted that. The love I have for you is real. I never meant to hurt you, Poetry. I've been trying to make it right for months and you have shut me out at every turn."

"Montez, how the hell did this go from this baby to all the shit you have done? This ain't about you! I still don't want to hear any of that mess. I still don't forgive you for cheating on me. If you think a baby will make me forget, you are sadly mistaken. This baby will not bring us back together because there won't be a baby," I said, getting angry.

"Poe, you are not killing my baby! That's out of the question. I will do everything in my power to make sure y'all are straight. I'm begging you, please think about this before you make a decision. I can't tell you what to do with your body, so I'm sorry for raising my voice. All I want you to do is think about me, about us," he said with tears in his eyes.

"I have plans and goals, Montez. A baby was not filtered into any of that. My parents are not about to go for this baby shit. Hell, I'm not going for it either. I'm sorry if this is going to hurt you, but I'm not having this baby. Yeah, you said you got us, and I believe you. I want to be able to provide for my child, as well. I can't give you that much power over me. Back in Chicago, I had a job. I didn't rely on you to take care of me. The things you did was because you wanted to do them, not because I needed you to. I'm not ready for a baby."

"Okay, Poe. You are not ready for a baby. I heard you several times already. Are you gon' consider me in this shit?"

"I have to talk to my parents," I said as a knock sounded at the door.

"It's time for us to see the little peanut! Are you guys excited? You must be the father," Dr. McCoy asked Montez, pushing the ultrasound machine into the room.

"Yeah, I am," he responded dry as hell.

Dr. McCoy set up his equipment and Monty and I were quiet the entire time. The excitement of being pregnant just wasn't there. My college life hadn't even started and I'd already started off on the wrong foot. I had let myself down and I was disappointed.

"Alright, I will apply this gel on your stomach, so lay back for me and raise your shirt, Miss Parker. It will be a little cold, but the image on the screen will warm you up, I promise," he said, smiling.

Slowly raising my shirt, I waited for Dr. McCoy to do what he was trained to do. He applied the gel and it was cold just like he said it would be. As he moved a wand-like object over my belly, I stared at the screen but didn't see anything.

"There we go," he said, pointing at the small image that appeared on the screen.

It looked like a little peanut sitting inside a bubble. I could see plain as day that there was truly a baby nestling in my womb. The tears fell from the corner of my left eye and I felt Montez wipe it away with his finger. He grasped my hand and gave it a gentle squeeze.

Dr. McCoy clicked the mouse and a loud galloping sound filled the room. "That's a strong heartbeat! It sounds good," he said excitedly. "There's only one baby," he said, laughing.

"One is more than enough," I mumbled.

Montez squeezed my hand again, while rubbing his thumb over the back of it. My eyes were trained on the screen and my heart was beating faster than usual. In my mind I thought, *"I can't have this baby."* But my emotions were in overdrive from seeing the life I helped create before my eyes.

"You're scanning at eight weeks along in this pregnancy. Everything looks really good, thus far. Such a healthy baby. Black is fluid," Dr. McCoy started to explain, pointing at the screen. "That would be your bladder with no fluid. This is your uterus with amniotic fluid with the little bean inside."

As he moved the wand around, parts of the little body could be seen. I looked up at Montez and he was smiling from ear to ear now that he knew what he was seeing. It melted my heart for only a quick second, then my mental thoughts kicked in again.

"I would put your due date around the March range and the heartbeat is at one hundred seventy beats per minute. Like I said, everything is looking pretty good from what I see," he said, clicking on the mouse. "Oh, the baby moved a little bit! It's unusual for the baby to move at eight weeks. It usually starts about nine weeks or so. I've snapped several pictures and they will be printing out soon. Other than that, we are all done today. I will set you up with an OBGyn appointment. It will be in a month," he said, wiping my stomach.

Montez took the paper towel from him and finished the deed. I could see he was going to be watching me like a hawk. Being around him was something I didn't want to do. He had really hurt me and this baby would not change that one bit.

"Is it too late for an abortion?" I asked before I realized what I had asked. Montez hand went still and the room got deathly quiet.

"Um, no actually it's not too late to terminate, but is that something you are considering?" Dr. McCoy asked.

"Nah, she ain't considering that shit," Montez cut in.

"Yes, I am. How much time do I have to make my decision, doctor?" Montez stood and I could feel the hole he was burning in the side of my face.

"Here in Georgia, majority of abortions take place before twelve weeks. However, most outpatient clinics offer abortions up to twenty weeks."

"Dr. McCoy, she don't need to know any of that. Poetry, would you please reconsider this please? Didn't you hear the heartbeat of our baby? It's a human being in there and you are considering killing it!"

I was trying to tune out Montez's plea, but the hurt in his voice was getting to me. "Montez, please. I have to talk to my parents about this. I'm trying to weigh my options, okay."

"I'll be back with your appointments, prescription, and discharge papers. You guys should really talk about this situation. I'll leave you all alone to give you time to discuss things."

Dr. McCoy hurried out of the room and I wiped the remaining gel from my stomach. Getting off the bed, I put my shoes on and started pacing back and forth. The only thing on my mind was getting rid of this baby.

"Poe, —"

"Save it! When it's all said and done, the choice is mine. This is my body and I have control of it."

"You right, but that's my baby, too! This is something we should decide together. You are being very selfish right now!" Montez yelled at me.

The door opened and Jonathan walked in without notice. "I can hear the two of you out in the hall. This is not the place to discuss this for everyone to hear. Save it until y'all are alone in private. I won't lecture neither one of you on this matter. Both of you are grown and this is the time for y'all to act like it."

Jonathan walked out without another word and soon after, Dr. McCoy walked back in with everything I needed in hand. I signed off on the paperwork and put the prescriptions in my pocket. Walking out without looking back at Montez, I met Kaymee and Jonathan in the hall.

"Can I ride with y'all? My truck is still on campus. I need to get something to eat and lay down for a while," I asked Jonathan.

"Sure. What do you want to eat? Give me your keys too so I can get the truck back to the house."

"Anything, it really doesn't matter and Kaymee has my keys," I said as I walked toward the exit.

"Poe!" Montez yelled at my back.

"I'll talk to you later, Montez. I don't feel like arguing about this right now."

Continuing to walk, I went out the door and the tears rolled down my face as I spotted Jonathan's car close to the entrance. Kaymee came out and embraced me in a hug, rubbing my back.

"I can't have a baby right now, Mee. I think I should get an abortion."

"If you are looking for me to agree with you, I won't do it. That's a decision you and Monty have to make amongst y'all. Talk to your parents and calm down first. The way you and Monty were yelling at each other, I think a day or two is needed before y'all try to talk about this subject again. Come on, let's get in the car. My daddy is talking to Monty, so it may be a minute," she said, holding my hand as we walked to the car.

Chapter 8
Montez

Poetry had me in a place I'd never wanted to be, in a position to choke the fuck out of her. It hurt me to know she didn't want to have the baby, but when she asked the doctor about abortions, I was done. Begging and pleading with her was overlooked and I took that as 'fuck what you talking 'bout, nigga.'

She had the nerve to ignore me when I tried to talk to her. I was following her out the door when Jonathan grabbed me by the arm. It took everything in me not to snatch away from his ass, but the glare he threw my way stopped me from reacting.

"Give her time, man. You have to understand that she is still young. She is probably worried about how her parents are going to react to the news of her being pregnant. I know you will do right by her and the baby, at least I hope you will," he said, looking at me sternly. "Poetry is scared, Montez. She came to Atlanta to further her education so she could better her life. Finding out that she's carrying a baby is something that wasn't in the plans. Just give her time to process the news about the baby."

"She is only doing this shit because we ain't together. It's not like I haven't tried to make things right. I've apologized for the shit I did and even told her the bitch didn't mean anything to me. Her ass ain't trying to hear none of what I've said! Now she wants to kill my fuckin' seed on some vindictive shit and you want me to give her space to go to the muthafuckin' clinic! Nah, I don't think I can do that," I said, punching the wall.

"Did you hear anything I just said to you, boy? Get out yo' feelings before you really lose that girl. I don't know what the fuck you did to her and I don't care. But if you want her back, you better listen to what I just told you. Poetry don't seem like the type of female that will do something out of spite. I see a very mature young woman that is determined to be something in life. You better try to do everything in your power to make it right before you be watching her life flourish from the sideline. I'm done trying to get you to see the bigger picture, you're on your own," Jonathan said, walking away from me.

I stood in the hall a bit longer thinking about what Jonathan had said. I pushed off the wall and walked toward the waiting room. Los was waiting for me by the door with a confused expression. He opened his mouth to say something and I held my hand up and shook my head, leading the way out of the hospital.

"Damn, man. What the fuck happened?" he asked.

"I don't want to talk about it right now, Los. Poetry is good if that's what you're worried about."

"Look, I heard what Jonathan said to you. I think he's right, fam. Just give her a minute. I know you are hot about the abortion thing, but I've been there done that. The difference is the girl that did that shit to me, did it to hurt me. I don't think Poetry would do something like that behind your back. She will talk to you about the situation. Let her be for the moment."

My phone started vibrating on my hip and I pulled it off my hip. "What up?" I paused as I listened. "Yeah, I'll be there in thirty," I said, ending the call. "Aye, follow me to the crib. I'm gon' leave you there to sort out the merch while I go make this drop. Is that cool?" I asked Los.

"Yeah, I'm with that."

"A'ight, let's go get this money."

I jumped in my whip and Los got in his. As I drove out of the parking lot, my phone rang again and Mena's name appeared on the radio display. Why she was calling, I didn't know. But she hadn't gotten any play on my phone since the day she broke Mee's window back in Chicago. Ignoring the call, I kept driving towards my apartment with my mind on Poetry and our baby.

It was hard to be happy about the pregnancy knowing she wanted to get rid of the baby. I wasn't a praying nigga, but I was silently asking God to help her do the right thing. Poetry was the love of my life and I really fucked up when I messed around with Mena. The blame for all of that was solely on me. That was one thing I was going to regret for the rest of my life if I lost Poetry. She had been making it very clear that she was done with me, so I knew a baby wouldn't change any of that.

When I pulled up to my crib, I saw that nigga Dray's ride parked. My blood boiled because I told this nigga to get the fuck out of my shit. Throwing my car in park, I hopped out and stormed up the stairs. As I pulled my keys out, the door swung open and Dray was coming out with boxes in his arms.

"Oh, my bad," he said, stepping aside.

"I hope that's your shit because I told you to get the fuck out."

"Yep, I'll be out in no time," he said, walking past me and out the door.

I looked around the room and noticed he had several boxes packed and stacked by the door. Walking to the room that used to be his, I peeked in and the only thing in there was his dressers and bed. He had to have all his shit out by nightfall or it was going to the garbage.

Leaving the doorway, I went back through the living room and out the door to my car. I popped the drunk and grabbed the duffel bag. Los stood waiting for me but kept his eyes on Dray as he loaded his truck with boxes. We went back into my apartment and I sat the bag on the table and disappeared into my room.

Coming back out, I had a scale and baggies in hand so Los could get to work on the product. I also had the package that I had to drop off in a bookbag. Dray entered the apartment and glanced in our direction with a scowl on his face.

"How long will it take you to get yo' shit out of here?" I asked without looking at him. "I have work to do and you and your boxes are in the way."

"As fast as I can seeming that I'm moving everything by myself."

"I'll help you, man," Los volunteered.

"Nah, I got," he said, picking up more boxes and leaving out the door.

"Man, he may be a problem," Los said.

"He won't be. Dray acts hard, but he ain't gon' pull that trigga. Not with me anyway. He better keep spooking Kaymee's ass and he gon' cut that shit short, too."

"Speaking of Kaymee, is she done with that nigga?" Los asked slyly.

Dray walked in the apartment at that precise moment and the venom dripped from his lips. "Hell naw, she ain't done with me! Respect my shit, Los and stay the fuck away from her!"

"Pipe that shit down, nigga! If she knew what I know, she would run away from yo' ass. You don't deserve my muthafuckin' sister. I'm hoping like hell she wakes up before it's too late."

"I can't believe you letting my relationship come between the bond we had—"

Shutting his ass up quickly, I went in on him. "When it comes to my family, muthafucka, all bets are off. I'm not gon' sit back and watch you fuck over her. If the bond was so strong between us, you would've known to treat her like the queen she was destined to be. Instead, you acting like a fuck nigga. So, you just made it possible for me to *tell* her to stop fuckin' with yo punk ass," I said, walking up on him.

"Nah, Monty. Let this nigga get his shit so he can move around," Los said, stopping me from approaching him.

"I'm not worried about you telling her shit, fam. Her heart belongs to me and she won't believe shit you gotta say. If she don't see for herself, it didn't happen," he said with a smirk. "The shit she saw the other day, I already got her believing it wasn't what she thought. She will forever be mine whether you like it or not. I'll be back for the rest of my shit later today," he said, picking up the last of the boxes.

"Don't come back to this muthafucka! All you don't get now, you won't be gettin', nigga. I don't give a fuck if you got to move the shit on yo' back! Get it up outta here, now! As a matter of fact, drop my fuckin' keys before you slide," I said, staring him in the eyes.

"I'll leave the keys after I get the rest of my shit, Monty! I'm not yo' bitch and you ain't about to keep talking to me like I'm one either," Dray said, dropping the boxes on the floor.

"Square the fuck up, nigga! You dropped that shit like you 'bout to do some damage. Yo' ass don't want these problems with me, Dray," I said, walking up on him.

"I'm not even about to go there with you, fam. Keep that shit in the other room, I'll buy another bedroom set," he said, removing the keys from his keyring. "Remember, I was that nigga that had yo' back."

Dray tossed the keys at my feet and I tried to knock his head off his shoulders. I didn't know who the fuck he thought I was, but he had the game all the way fucked up. Los jumped in between us and pushed me back towards the kitchen.

"Fuck you, Dray! Stay the hell away from me and Kaymee, nigga! You better pray she don't come back and tell me you doing her any dirtier than you already have!"

He scooped up the boxes and left out of the apartment without looking back. I wanted to kill his ass, but he was going to dig his own grave in due time. My chest was heaving in and out and I felt my body temperature rising. I had to make Kaymee see that Dray was not the man for her. He had too much muthafuckin' baggage.

I snatched my phone off my hip and hit Kaymee's name. She answered on the second ring, "Hey, bro. Poetry don't want to talk to you right now."

"I'm not trying to holla at Poe. You're who I need to speak with, Mee. I want you to stay away from Dray. Whatever he has said in order for him to clear his name, don't believe none of that shit."

"Monty, I love you like a brother, but let me handle Dray. He has a lot to prove if he wants to be with me and only me. What I saw was disrespectful as hell. There's no way he can tell me it wasn't what it was."

"I feel like I need to fill you in on what's really going on with him. I tried to stay out of it, but I refuse to let him play you. Alexis is not his only problem," I said, pausing. "Mee, Dray is about to be a father. If you're ready to deal with baby mama drama, as well as him constantly lying, then go for it. I don't want you to think I've been holding back secrets because I haven't. I gave him the opportunity to come clean with the shit and he didn't. I've cut all ties with his ass and I'd advise you to do the same before I kill that nigga."

Kaymee was quiet for a few seconds, then she mumbled to herself, "A baby? How can he have a whole baby on the way? I'm going to confront him about this. I won't mention your name, though. Thank you for always looking out for me, Monty. I don't know what I'd do without you."

"Stop thanking me for doing what I signed up for. We are and always will be family. I hate that I introduced his ass to you."

"It's not your fault I fell in love with a lying, cheating, abuser. Fuck Dray, with his psychotic ass!" she yelled.

I didn't think Kaymee realized what she'd let slip out of her mouth. Anger took over and she just went off. "Mee, what do you mean by abuser?" I asked angrily.

"Monty, don't jump off the deep end. He hasn't put his hands on me or anything. It's just the tone of voice he used and what he actually said," she tried to explain.

"Nah, you already let the cat out the bag. That mutha-fucka threatening you? Don't lie either because I'm not standing for you covering up for him, Kaymee. Tell me what his pussy ass said to you."

"I'll handle this my way, please. I don't want to involve you or anyone else for that matter. Would you keep this between us? That means don't go running your mouth to Jonathan. Dray and I will have a conversation about this shit. If he lies, I'm done."

I couldn't believe she was giving this nigga that much leverage to keep playing her. Kaymee thought she had this shit under control and all I could do was step back and allow her to handle it. The time for me to step up will come eventually and I would be ready. I didn't like the fact that she was acting like one of them airhead bitches that I tried my best to stay away from.

“A’ight, Mee. You got that. I’m gon’ keep my mouth closed from this point on. Do what you feel you gotta do. I’ll holla at you later. I have business to take care of. Hit me on the horn if you need me. Tell Poe I love her,” I said, hanging up.

It defeated the purpose of trying to school her ass, on the real. She was letting her pussy speak for her and she was going to get hurt in the end. I would be there to help her through it all, but this was going to be a hard lesson learned. ‘I told you so’ will be on the tip of my tongue when everything hits the fan.

“I’m out, Los. If that nigga comes back, don’t let him in my shit. I’ll be back within the hour,” I said, leaving out the door with the backpack slung over my shoulder.

Chapter 9
Dot

"Where are these fools? They're usually out here in front of this damn building like a pack of wolves!"

I talked to myself as I scanned the streets for the local dealers that were always outside when I needed them. The crack was calling me ferociously. My body was craving it and I found myself chasing the same high I got the first time I smoked the shit. It was nowhere to be found. Jonathan was going to get his. I knew he was the one that did this to me. I would never do drugs willingly, so it had to be in the weed he left in my house the day he and G barged in my shit.

I'd been walking the streets for hours, trying to find my next hit. I was scratching like the fiends I used to laugh and talk about without a dime to my name. I kept pulling my pants up because I had lost so much weight, they were falling down with every step I took. The person I had been looking for emerged from the corner store talking on his phone. I got happy as hell.

"Aye, D!" I yelled loudly as I hiked my pants up and jogged up the street. "Yo, D!" I screamed again frantically when he didn't respond the first time.

D put his phone in his pocket and looked in my direction evilly. "What the fuck you want, Dot?" he asked nastily as I approached him out of breath.

"I need some blow," I forced out, breathing heavily.

"You know where to find me when it comes to that!" he said, opening the door to his car.

"I've been waiting for you for the longest, so I started walking around looking for you."

"Bitch, if I'm not at the spot, sit yo' ass in the window and wait until I get there! Don't be hounding me down like I owe yo' ass something! You probably ain't got no damn money any fuckin' way!"

I hated when he talked to me like I wasn't shit. D thought he was the shit since he joined the Goon Squad. I think he had a hand in Joe getting killed so they could take over his shit, but that wasn't my business.

"You know I'm good for it, D. I'll get it to you as soon as my man comes in tonight. I need that right now. I'm sick," I all but pleaded.

"Get the fuck outta her with that bullshit, Dot," he said, walking back to the curb where I stood. "I'm still waiting on you to pay me back for the other pack I gave yo' ass. What happened to you paying me back for that?" he asked, putting his hands in his pockets.

"I—I paid you back for that," I stuttered.

"You a muthafuckin' lie! I'm not giving you shit. If you can't pay to get high, that's something you don't need to be doing, right?"

"Come on, D! I'm gon' pay you back I promise," I begged. "Let's work it off in a special way."

I was trying to put on my sexy voice that worked with many men back in the day. I didn't care how desperate it made me look. I needed those drugs. Whatever I had to do, I was all for it.

D laughed at me while looking around to see who was within earshot. He walked close to me and scrunched up his nose. "If you ever suggest fuckin' me, I'll shoot yo' ass between the eyes," he growled. "Get the fuck away from me, Dot. Holla at me when you got some money."

Watching him get in his car and drive off, made me want to cry. I'd been walking and I was tired as hell and it was for nothing because I still needed to get high. As I stood there looking dumb, I started walking back toward my house.

While walking, I decided to detour and take a scroll onto Michigan Avenue.

It took me about twenty minutes to make my way to the corner of Chicago Avenue and Michigan. I picked up a used cup because the only way I would be able to get some money was by panhandling. These folks down here would drop money in a heartbeat and I was here to receive whatever they were willing to give.

I stood in front of the Nieman Marcus store shaking my cup at everyone that passed. "Can you help me out with some change, please?" The first ten minutes were pissing me off because all I got were looks of disgust from these damn people. How dare them look at me like I wasn't a human fuckin' being.

After about twenty minutes, I had about five dollars and that wasn't nearly enough. Frustration was starting to kick in and another tactic entered my mind. If they didn't want to help me out, then I didn't have a choice but to take what I wanted. Scoping out a target, I didn't see one that was going to be an easy hit. So, I went back to shaking my cup.

A young girl walked passed me with her wallet hanging out of her pocket. I knew that was my one and only chance to come up. Rushing forward, I maneuvered through the crowd until I was directly behind her. An impatient man bumped into her at the exact time I reached for her wallet, forcing her into me. Her wallet was in my pocket before she could turn in my direction and hurriedly moved away from.

I didn't give a fuck because I had what I needed. Briskly walking back to Chicago Avenue, I headed home with a smile on my face. Once I got a safe distance away, I opened the wallet to see what kind of come up I lucked up on. There were a lot of bills inside, along with a couple of credit cards, and a monthly bus pass. I took that as a blessing because the bus was stopped at the light a block away and I would be on it.

Standing at the bus stop when the bus pulled up, I stepped on and scanned my card. Going straight to the back, I sat down and counted the money in the wallet. That little bitch had four hundred and eighty dollars in a wallet that was hanging out of her pocket. I couldn't wait to get back so I could get a hundred dollars' worth of dope.

I had a few stops before I got off, so I pocketed the money, took the cards and the bus pass, and left the wallet under the seat. Pulling the cord to alert the driver that I wanted to get off, I took a hundred dollars from my stash and held it in my hand. D was standing outside when I exited the bus and I damn near flew over to him.

"Let me get a hundred worth," I said, smiling.

"Yo' ass gon' get beat the fuck up, Dot. I hope you didn't steal from the wrong muthafucka," he said, going around the side of the building to get my shit.

I wasn't trying to hear shit he was saying. His only concern should've been his money and not what I had to do to get it. Waiting patiently for him to come back, I was hopping from one foot to the other. I was anxious to get in the house and get high. D came back around the corner and slipped what I needed in my hand.

Opening my hand to make sure I had the right amount, I noticed he only gave me eighty dollars' worth. "D, you shorted me," I said, glaring at him.

"You got amnesia now? You owe me from last time. We just talked about this early. Take yo' ass on somewhere before you come up missin', Dot. By the way, Earl looking for yo' ass. He will be up to yo' apartment later," he said, walking away.

I hurried into the building and took the stairs to my place. Earl was the manager of the building. I had been avoiding him for the past month. When he come to my door today, he still wasn't gon' get an answer. I didn't have any damn money for his ass.

Unlocking the door, I rushed in and locked it behind me. I went straight to my room and prepared the first dose of my medicine. My hands were shaking with anticipation as I snatched my pipe out of the top drawer of my night stand. As I placed a small piece of crack inside and grabbed my lighter, my mouth watered. I'd been waiting to get high all damn day and I was ready.

The first puff went straight to my head and I held the smoke in longer than usual to get the full effect. My body instantly relaxed and I was in a zone. I finished the rock and reached for another. I was going to smoke until my lips were numbed because I wanted to be high high.

Boom! Boom! Boom!

Who the fuck was knocking on my shit like the fucking police? I couldn't get up fast enough before I heard my front door opening without me letting whoever it was in on the other side. Throwing the pipe in the drawer along with my stash, I stormed to the front of my apartment and stopped in my tracks when Earl rounded the wall.

"Dot, I know damn well you were told that I've been looking for your ass! Why you didn't answer the door?" Earl asked with an attitude.

"You didn't give me the opportunity to open the damn door, for one. Two, who the hell told you to come in my place? And last but not least—"

"Yo' ass got to raise up outta here," Earl said, cutting me off. "I've been chasing you for months to get the rent and you've been dodging me at all costs. I'm done chasing you,

Dot. This apartment is nasty as fuck! You have been smoking that shit in here, and you haven't paid shit! It's funny you have money to get high, but can't pay what you owe. Your time is up," he said, handing me a letter of eviction.

Reading over the letter the best I could through hazy eyes, all I focused on was the red letters that basically said I had to be out by September first. It was already the thirtieth of August. There was no way I could lose my place right before it was set to get cold outside. Chicago was brutal during the winter.

"Earl, come on. This is sudden. What happened to a thirty-day notice? This is illegal as hell and y'all can't put me out two days before the date!" I screamed.

"Dot, look at the date on that paper. I didn't just write this up yesterday and decided to bring it to you today. You are the reason I didn't get it in your hands before now. On top of that, I gave you two warning letters before this one was even filed. Don't give me the sob story about doing you wrong either because I don't want to hear it."

"Well how much will I have to pay to prevent this?" I asked in a shaky voice.

"Dot, you owe nine hundred dollars."

"Nine hundred! How is that? My rent was a hundred dollars a month, where the hell all the tax come from? Y'all trying to get over on me!"

"Your daughter turned eighteen in May. Once that happened, you were no longer eligible for the low-income rate. We go according to your income now," he explained to me. I wasn't trying to hear that though because it was bullshit.

"What income do I have, Earl? I don't have a muthafuckin' job, so my rent should be zero! Ya'll on some bullshit, but I will be getting a lawyer because this is wrong on all levels."

"Social security is a form of income, just in case you didn't know, Dot," he chuckled. "What you're getting it for is not my concern. Just know that we're aware of it."

I didn't know how they found out about that and I didn't have a comeback for him. In my mind, I was trying to figure out how to buy some time so I could stay in my place. "Let me fuck the payment off, Earl," I threw at him, praying he caught the bait.

His ass had the nerve to laugh in my face and it pissed me off even more. "Dot, if you ran into these problems back in the day, I would've worked that out with you. Baby girl, you have fell the fuck off and I wouldn't stick you with some other niggas dick, ma. Yo' body ain't what it used to be, so that would be a no for me. If you can come up with the money, let me know tomorrow and I will make sure the eviction is lifted. Until then, it stands," he said, walking toward the door. "You know how to reach me if you come up with a solution."

"The only solution I have, you dismissed. I don't have anything else for you," I said to his back as he made his exit.

Knowing that I was about to be evicted had me paranoid. I'd burned bridges with everybody that had been there with me throughout the years and I had no one to turn to. Instead of dwelling on my situation, I went back to my room and picked up my glass dick and continued to get high.

After smoking four rocks to the head, I was finally in the mindset to make a few calls to see if I could get this money. The three hundred I had from my lick was still an option if I couldn't get someone to give me the whole nine hundred.

The first person I called was Dame, but he must've still had me blocked. The call went straight to voicemail. I knew I couldn't call Stan's ass. After I hit his ass upside his head with my piece, he changed his number and I hadn't heard from him. I was pressing my luck trying to call a nigga named Bo. It had been years since I've even seen his ass, but he never changes his number.

Listening to the phone ring, I thought he wasn't going to answer but I was wrong. He answered right before the voicemail picked up. "Who dis?" his voice boomed through the earpiece.

"Hey, stranger. How have you been?" I asked sexily.

"Dot?" he asked uncertainly.

"Yeah, it's me. What's up with ya?"

"I'm good. What made you call me? I haven't talked to you in what, two or three years?"

"I didn't have anyone else to call. I'm in a bind and I was wondering if you could loan me nine hundred dollars. I'm on the verge of being evicted from my apartment," I said, faking a cry.

"Well, bitch, that's your problem! You have a lot of nerve calling my husband for money. He has a whole family and his money is tied up with shit that matters, his kids and me, his wife. Find you another nigga to swindle out of money. Don't call this muthafucka no more because whatever the fuck y'all had is a done deal. Lose this number and that's the last time I will be saying shit about the matter." Before I could say anything back, she hung up on me.

Calling Jonathan was out of the question because he wouldn't piss on my ass if I was on fire. The thought came and went because I knew who he would give the money to and that lil' bitch owed me her fucking life. I dialed Kaymee's number and she sent me to voicemail. She was not about to ignore me like I was one of her friends. I called back and got the same results. So, being the petty one, I kept calling until she answered.

"What is it, Dot?" she asked irritably.

"Is that how you answer the phone for your mother?"

"You haven't been a mother to me in a long time. Again, what is it, Dot?"

I wanted to curse her ass out, but I had to hold my tongue because she had something that I needed. The approach I wanted to take had to go on the back burner for now. Being nice was something I had to pull out of my bag of tricks in order for her to hear me out.

"I can't call to see how you've been? I'm only trying to make sure you are doing alright down there."

"Since when have you been worried about my wellbe-ing? Let's cut the shit and get to the real reason you're on my phone, Dot?"

"You will not use that tone of voice with me, let alone cussin' at me like I'm not your mother! Show some respect, Kaymee!"

"Respect? Do you even know what the word means? Is respect when I sat back while you talked to me like I didn't mean anything to you? Or was is it when you allowed your boyfriend to molest me with his eyes and you called me a whore? Maybe it was when you would beat my ass and called me out my name for all the mistakes you made. No wait, maybe it was when you shot me! I showed respect by not beating yo' ass! Now I'm going to respect you by ending this call because I don't have too much to say to you."

"Kaymee, wait! Don't hang up, please! I need your help. I'm about to be evicted from my apartment and I have nowhere to go. I need nine hundred dollars or I will be put out on the streets. Please help your mother out, baby," I pleaded.

"That's so ironic," she laughed. "I've always wanted you to be a loving mother that talked to me in this tone of voice, but I 've never gotten that got from you. All of a sudden you need my help after all the years I needed you! God don't like ugly, Dot. You reap what you sow. As for you being my mother, I will let you know if I can help you. Right now, I need to get off this phone before I change my mind about even considering helping you," she said.

"Bitch, what is there to consider? It's either you gon' help me or you're not! There's no need to prolong your answer! I'm your mother and you owe me, Kaymee!"

There was a long silence on the other end of the phone. "Did you hear what I said?" When I didn't get a response, I looked down at the phone and my home screen was on display. Her ass hung up on me and I knew then I had fucked up my only chance of keeping my place.

Chapter 10
Kaymee

The day had finally come for me to get the cast taken off my arm. I was sitting in the waiting room of the hospital, waiting for my name to be called. It had been a few days since Dot called asking for help with her bills. I was truly going to help her because I didn't want my mother getting put out. She killed all possibilities when she converted back to her old self. All she had to do was agree to disagree nicely and the money was hers. But nooo, she had to let the hate she had for me show its face.

I ignored every call thereafter and eventually put her on the block list. I talked to Jonathan about it and he informed me that Dot was on drugs. Hearing him say that hurt like hell because I couldn't believe she had stooped so low in her life. That was the reason I was going hard for myself because I didn't want to end up in that predicament. I would never depend on anyone to do anything for me.

"Kaymee Morrison."

Hearing my name brought me out of my train of thought. I grabbed my bag and stood from the chair I was sitting in and walked toward the nurse that had called my name. She led me to a room and told me the doctor would be in shortly. When I climbed onto the bed, my phone chimed, indicating I had a text message. I got comfortable and pulled my phone out of my purse and checked the message.

Dray: Wyd?

I read that shit and went straight to my social media account. I didn't have two words to say to that man. The way he was talking to me, threatening me like he owned me, was something I wasn't about to deal with. The things Monty told me about Dray had been on my mind constantly. I'd yet to talk to him about the information that I had, but I planned on doing it very soon.

Going through all the things I did with Dot, was something I didn't want to convert back to in a relationship with someone that claimed they loved me. This love thing was new to me and Dray was the first man I'd been with. As much as I wanted to give him a chance to redeem himself, I didn't think things would be better. He had already shown me what type of man he could be from both angles.

There were two soft knocks on the door and the doctor walked in with a machine that looked like a vacuum cleaner. "Hello, Kaymee. I'm Dr. Lucas and I will be removing your cast today. How are you?" he asked as he plugged the machine into the wall.

"I'm fine. Thanks for asking. I can't wait to get this thing off. I'm tired of not being able to scratch my arm," I said, laughing.

"I do understand. Let me explain what I will be doing today. This is called a cast saw. It is going to be pretty loud because it's connected to the vacuum so the dust will not fly over the room. It will not hurt you at all. It's not the type of saw from the shed and it is very safe for us to use. You will not lose a limb," he joked. He picked up a pair of scissors and held them up. "Once I cut the cast with the saw, I will use these safe scissors to finish cutting the cast from your arm. Are you ready to do this?" he asked, looking at me.

"Yes, I'm so ready," I responded, grabbing my phone to record the process.

"You young folks have to record everything nowadays I see."

"I'm doing it to remember what I had to go through. It's for myself," I explained to him.

Dr. Lucas started the saw and like he said, it was pretty loud but not scary. As he started cutting a line along the cast, the vibrations tickled, making me laugh out loud. He looked up at me and chuckled.

"Yes, I forgot to tell you that it would tickle. Try not to move too much for me, Kaymee."

He moved to the other side and started a line identical to the previous one. There was a strong odor that hit me, making me gag a little bit. I held my right hand over my nose because I couldn't believe my arm smelled like musty ass.

Dr. Lucas turned the saw off so I could hear him speak. "The distinct odor is normal. Your arm has been covered for two months without being washed. The skin that sheds on our arms can't be seen in everyday living but when it's covered, it falls inside the cast with nowhere to go. Don't worry, I'll tell you how to care for it before you leave here."

Turning the saw back on, he ran it over the line a couple more times before he cut the saw off again. He then picked up the scissors and began cutting the cast open. I got a glimpse of my arm and it was hairy as hell. The hair on my arm was thicker than usual. Once the cast was loosened, he pulled it off my arm.

"Oh wow! My arm is so skinny compared to my right one. My skin is so scaly and dry. How long will it take for my arm to go back to the size it used to be?"

"Well, your muscles are weak from not being used. It will take a little while to get back to normal. I want you to take it easy during this time. As far as your dry skin, you may be tempted to scratched or scrub all the dead skin off—don't. For the first few days, I want you to soak your arm in warm water for twenty minutes twice a day. Gently pat your skin dry with a soft towel.

You don't want to rub hard because you don't want to damage the new skin. Use a fragrance-free lotion to keep your skin soft. Lotions made with cocoa butter works well. Do you have any questions for me?" I shook my head no. "Okay. We will head over to X-ray to make sure this baby is healed properly," he said, leading me out of the room.

It didn't take long at all to get the x-rays done. Everything looked good according to what Dr. Lucas saw on the screen. When we got back to the room, everything he explained to me was already printed out along with my discharge papers.

"Do you want to keep your cast, Kaymee?"

"No, you guys can have that. I'm happy to get rid of that thing."

"Okay, I will be right back. You will have to wear a brace on your arm for a couple weeks until your muscles are stronger to protect that arm," he said leaving the room.

Once he came back, he helped me put on the brace. I thanked Dr. Lucas and bounced out of the room happily. Riding down on the elevator, I kept looking at my arm and it felt so light. Wearing that cast felt like I was carrying three extra pounds. The doors to the elevator opened and I stepped off. I hadn't eaten, so I decided to go to the Subway in the cafeteria to grab a sandwich.

Ordering a six-inch sub on wheat, a bag of chips and a drink, I decided to eat there. Finding a place to sit, I pulled out my phone and there was another text from Dray. I took a bite of my sandwich before I even attempted to see what he was talking about. When I opened the text, I knew then that he was out of his mind.

Dray: I thought I made it clear that when I called or text, you answer! It didn't mean look at my shit and say fuck me!

Kaymee, you are really trying to make me lay hands on your ass I see.

I didn't reply to that message either because I didn't feel the need to. He needed to calm his ass down. He was the one that got caught with his hands and mouth on another woman, not me. I would talk to him when I was ready. Not on his terms.

The cafeteria wasn't crowded and it was pretty quiet. I was reading a book on my kindle called *XYZ* by this new author named Kimille and it was getting good as hell. The doors to the cafeteria opened and I automatically looked up. I couldn't believe what the fuck I saw. Dray was walking hand and hand with a woman that appeared to be pregnant, but he was texting me talking shit. I put my kindle away and closed my food up, putting it in my purse.

I sat watching their interaction for about five minutes and couldn't take it anymore. Rising from the chair I was sitting in, I slung the strap of my purse over my shoulder and headed in their direction. He wasn't expecting to see me so when I stood behind them like I was waiting to place an order, neither of them turned around.

"It was exciting to finally see my baby on the screen," he said, smiling from ear to ear. "When the heartbeat came through the speakers, I almost cried. Don't say shit, Melody." He smiled, looking like a man in love.

"Your baby, huh?" I blurted out.

Dray turned around with a shocked expression on his face. "Kay—Kaymee! What are you doing here?" he asked nervously.

"The question isn't why I'm here. What the fuck are you doing here? You have the nerve to text me talking shit about me not responding to you while you're sitting looking at a baby on an ultrasound machine. It looks like you were texting me about the wrong shit. What ya should've been doing was telling me about the baby you have on the way. Don't worry about it, though. I'm done," I said, turning to walk away.

Dray grabbed me by my arm and I looked down at his hand. He didn't release me, so I snatched away from his punk ass. Mad was an understatement. I was furious and wanted to slap the taste out his mouth. But I learned from the girls in high school not to hit a man without expecting to get hit back.

"Let me explain, baby," he said, trying to push me away from the girl he was with. I wasn't trying to hear none of that shit he was spitting.

"There's nothing you can say to make this right. You have a baby on the way and I'm not trying to be step mama to someone I didn't push out my own pussy. Go back over there and make that shit work with your baby mama. You and I are done, Dray. Don't call me anymore. We don't have anything tying us together," I said, walking out on him.

I pulled my keys out of my pocket to unlock the doors of my new hunter green BMW 530e that my daddy finally bought me. Taking a step out of the hospital doors, I felt a hand grabbed the back of my neck and forcing me further out of the door.

"You don't fuckin' embarrass me in public! Who do you think I am, Kaymee? I've already told yo' monkey ass we weren't breaking up because you said so," Dray snarled from behind me.

Reaching my arm back, I pried his hand from my neck and turned around quickly. The way his face was scrunched up, I could tell he was mad, but I didn't care. It was always about how he felt when he got caught up. He was the victim in the wrongdoings that he caused.

"Embarrassed? Dray you will not continue trying to turn the tables, making this my fault. Nigga, this is all you! If anybody is looking like a fool, it's me. You and all your hoes can live ya'll best lives. I don't want any parts of the bullshit. I have bigger and better things to worry about and you ain't about to be one of them. Now leave me the fuck alone!" I said, walking in the direction of my car.

"Bring yo' ass back here, Kaymee!" he yelled.

I ignored his ass and jumped in my car. Pushing the start button, I backed out the spot as my phone started ringing. I glanced at the display of my car and it was Dray calling. He could call until he turned blue in the face. He would never talk to me again on the line I paid for. "Drayton Montgomery could kiss my ass!" I yelled speeding down the street.

***

My class schedule was hectic, but I loved every bit of it. I was all about my school work and I was killing every class. It has been three weeks since the incident with Dray in the hospital. He continued calling my phone until I had to finally block him. Besides school, I was trying to be the best friend I could be to Poetry.

She was still scared about having a baby but with her parents on her side, she had come to terms with it. When she called her mother and told her what was going on, she cried the entire time and confessed that she wanted an abortion. Mama Chris told her that she was against abortions and didn't want her to do it.

Poetry hasn't told Monty that she wasn't going to abort the baby, but they have been communicating better than before. She removed him from the block list and answered his text messages every now and again. To me it was a start and I believed they were going to be alright.

I was sitting at my desk going over homework for my microbiology class. Poetry was at her late class and wouldn't be back until after seven. There was a knock on my door and I ignored it because I wasn't expecting anyone.

Bam! Bam! Bam!

Sighing, I got up and walked down the hall to the door. I looked out the peephole and Dray was standing on the other side. There was nothing to talk about because I was no longer his problem. He continued to knock hard on the door but I refused to open it, so I spoke to him through the door.

"What do you want, Dray?" I asked.

"Open the door. We need to talk."

"No, we don't. I said what I said back at the hospital and I meant every word. Now would you stop knocking on my door?"

"I'm not going anywhere until you open the door and talk to me!"

I could see where things were headed, so I went back to my room and grabbed my phone. I used the security app and summoned them to my dorm. If he didn't want to leave voluntarily, then I would have him removed. I didn't have time for his bullshit.

"You gon' fuck around and make me kick this mutha-fucka in! Now open this door!"

Dray was still in the hall screaming and hollering. I didn't say anything else to him and I was hoping security would hurry. With every minute that past, it seemed like he was getting angrier and angrier. Security finally showed up and tried to escort him out of the building, but he continued to refuse.

"My woman is in there and I'm not leaving until she talks to me! Don't fuckin' touch me, nigga!"

"I already called the police. I'm giving you the opportunity to leave before they get here, your choice," one of the guards said to Dray.

"I don't give a fuck who you called! I'm not leaving until I talk to my girl!" he said, knocking on the door again. "Kaymee, come on open the door. You got these bitches hounding me and shit. All you have to do is talk to me!"

I rolled my eyes toward the ceiling because what he wanted was not going to happen. When I said we were through, I meant that shit. I was living my life for me and it will be without the headache that I knew would come along with dealing with Dray.

I heard voices in the hall and a police officer identify himself. "Put your arms above your head, now!"

"I'm being harassed because I'm trying to see my girl? This is straight bullshit!" Dray screamed.

"Obviously, your girl doesn't want to see you. If she did, she wouldn't have called security over to make you leave. And since you are disturbing the peace, you are being arrested. Now I need you to put your hands behind your back," the officer said.

Dray must've done what they told him to do because I heard the handcuffs clicking around his wrists. Then there was a light knock on the door. Slowly walking to the door, I opened it and there was a police officer on the other side.

"Ma'am, are you okay?"

"Yes, I'm fine," I said.

"The guy says that you are his girlfriend. Is that true?"

"No, it's not true. I used to be his girlfriend until I broke up with him a couple weeks ago. I told him I was done and didn't want him calling me anymore. This was the first time

I've seen or talked to him since that day. I just want him to leave me alone," I explained to the officer.

"Well, he his going to jail tonight. You won't have anymore problems out of him. Here is a police report for tonight. If he continues to come here bothering you, or anywhere for that matter, get a restraining order and press charges. I have a feeling he will be back. Don't hesitate to call us as well as campus security, if needed. Have a goodnight," he said before leaving.

Closing and locking the door behind the officer, I went back to my room and laid down. Dray coming over acting a fool scared the hell out of me. I didn't know why he was acting this way when he was the reason behind everything that happened. He didn't want to talk until he got caught in a lie, then he wanted to show his aggressive side to scare me into being with him again.

I picked up my phone and called my daddy. "Hey, baby girl. How's school going?"

"Everything is going fine. I'm doing great in school. I just wanted to call and see how you were doing old man."

"Watch it with that old man shit, now," he said, laughing. "You haven't been by the house in a while. That makes me think you don't love me anymore."

"Now you know I love you, daddy! Speaking of that, I want you to know that I appreciate you with everything in me. Without you, I don't know where my mind would be."

"I'm not taking credit for that, Kaymee. You held your own long before I came back into your life. Pat yourself on the back for that. Without me, you would still be soaring high because that's what you want. Understand where I'm going with this. You hold your future in your hands. Don't give anybody credit over that. I'm only here to make sure you are on the right track and you don't need me for that either."

I was quiet for a moment, trying to decide if I wanted to tell him about what happened with Dray. I came to the conclusion not to because he would kill him and I needed my daddy out here with me, not in some damn prison. If Dray continued on the path he was on, I will fill my daddy in on everything. I just hoped it didn't come to that.

"I understand. How about Poetry and I come over tomorrow? Maybe we can catch a movie or something."

"Sounds good. I'll let Katrina know not to make plans so I can spoil my girls all at once. I won't hold you. It's Friday night and I'm quite sure you have plans with Dray."

"Daddy me and Dray are through. I have too much going on with myself to deal with the things he's bringing to the table. I'd rather do bad by myself. Don't ask any questions. I'll talk to you about it when I'm ready. Not today."

"Okay, baby. I'm here if you need me. Enjoy the rest of your night. I love you."

"I love you too, daddy," I said, hanging up.

Turning over in bed, I closed my eyes to rest them and ended up going to sleep.

Chapter 11
Montez

Driving on the highway, my mind kept drifted to Poetry. We were talking a little more than before, but it was basically me reaching out to her. When I would call, she didn't have much to say. But when I texted, she would talk forever. It was a start and I enjoyed the conversation however she gave it to me.

The subject of the baby was always the subject that cut communication short. I tried not to talk about it unless she brought it up. I wanted to be overly excited about her pregnancy, but I couldn't allow myself to do it. She was still riding the fence on what she wanted to do as far keeping the baby or getting an abortion. I wanted her to keep digging in her ass because the clock was ticking and fast, too. She was now almost twelve weeks. In no time, my baby would be moving around to capture her heart.

I talked her up because my phone rang mid thought and her name popped up on the display. Pushing the button, I answered quickly. "Hey, Poe," I said cheerfully.

"We need to talk," she said solemnly. The way she said those words made my heart drop. I didn't want to jump to conclusions, so I rolled with it.

"Is everything okay?"

"Yeah, I'm good. I just want to have this conversation before I change my mind. Would you meet me at the Starbucks around the corner from your apartment?"

"Why don't you just meet me at my apartment, Poe? I don't need everybody and their mama in my business."

"I think Starbucks will be a better option. I'll be there in fifteen minutes," she said, hanging up.

In my head, I was thinking she was about to tell me that she was going through with the abortion. The thought alone had me feeling some type of way and I knew, Starbucks wasn't the place to have that type of conversation. I headed to my apartment instead and parked.

As I walked inside my phone rang, it was Poe. "Come to my apartment, Poetry. I'm not discussing anything within earshot of other people. I'm here waiting on you, love," I said nicely.

"Montez, I told you to come to Starbucks! You always want things your way and I'm not for this shit today!"

"Please, just come to my place, Poe. I'm not trying to upset you, all I want is for us to be able to talk about whatever it is without eyes being on us," I tried to explain things to her and she wasn't going.

"It's either you meet me or I go my ass back to my dorm. As a matter of fact, don't worry about it."

"Poetry!" I yelled before she could hang up.

"What, Montez? I don't have time for all of this stupid ass back and forth shit."

"I'm on my way, okay? Hold tight. I'll be there in a minute."

She hung up and I ran my hand down my face. I knew I'd fucked up and it was up to me to make shit right. Even if it meant I had to bow down to the one I loved to a certain extent. Grabbing my keys, I decided to walk around the corner as I locked the door. When I entered the barista, I spotted Poetry sitting at a table in the back. She was glowing and her face was fuller. Her nose had spread a little bit but it looked cute.

Poetry looked up as I approached and she dropped the pastry that she was eating on a napkin. I pulled the chair out and hiked my pants up before I sat down. Folding my hands in front of me, I took in all of her beauty for a few seconds.

"Hey, I'm here. Are you gon' smile for a nigga?" I asked, trying to break the ice.

"Thank you for coming."

"What's on your mind, Poe?" I asked, never taking my eyes off her.

The frown on her face deepened as the seconds ticked away. I wasn't going to rush her into talking. Waiting patiently for her to say something, my phone rang. I didn't want to answer it because I knew it was about money. Looking down, I saw it was Los.

"What up?" I asked. Listening to him talk on the other end, I watched the expression on Poetry's face change from a frown to irritation. "Well, I'm gon' need you to handle that because I'm in the middle of an important meeting with Poetry right now. I'm not leaving until she's done talking." I could tell she was surprised when I made that statement. When money called, I was on it. It was a new day and I was changing things for her. "A'ight, I'll hit you when I'm done. Call me if you run into any problems, which I highly doubt."

"Sorry about that," I said as I laid my phone on the table. "Do you want something else to eat?"

"No, there isn't any food in this place. It's a snack," she said, laughing.

"Well, if you're hungry, we can go grab something to eat. What do you have a taste for? Seafood? Wanna go to Baltimore Crab and Seafood?" She smiled and I knew her mouth watered from the thought alone. Come on, let's go eat," I said, standing up.

Poetry grabbed her pastry and finished it off before she stood. Her stomach was started to protrude a bit and I smiled. It took everything in me not to reach out and rub my hand over it. Letting her walk ahead of me, I observed her from the back and I noticed her ass had gotten a little bigger, too.

"Mmh, mmh, mmh," I said, licking my licks.

She looked over my shoulder and shook her head. "Would you stop all that and come on? You got me wanting crab legs, lobster, and shrimp. I hope you brought your wallet," she said, laughing.

"My pockets stay fat, Poe. You can have the world if that's what you want," I shot back as we walked out the door.

"Where is your car? I don't feel like driving," she asked, looking up and down the street.

"I left it parked by the apartment and walked. You don't have to drive. Give me your keys."

That was right up her alley because she handed the keys to me and led me to her truck. I helped her inside and closed the door. Walking around to the other side, I got in and Poetry was watching every move I made. Pretending not to notice, I started the truck and pulled out into traffic. Neither one of us said anything for the first ten minutes, then Poetry decided to talk.

"I spoke to my parents about the baby," she said, glancing in my direction.

I looked at her long enough for her to know I heard her. Shit, I still had to drive. She's been around me long enough to know that I silently told her to continue, but she didn't right away. Biting her bottom lip, she sat quietly watching the scenery whisk by. Poetry was hesitating with whatever she was trying to tell me.

"What are you trying to say, love? Just let it out. Whatever it is, we will get through it together."

She took a deep breath and said, "I told them I was thinking about terminating the pregnancy, Monty," she said and paused.

My jaw clenched automatically. I was forcing myself to remain calm. The last thing I wanted to do was get angry with her. She was correct, I couldn't tell her what to do with her body. It didn't mean I wasn't hurt behind the shit. Not realizing how hard I was holding the steering wheel, let alone noticing the tear that fell from my eye.

"My mama was hurt, but she doesn't want me to get rid of the baby. She explained that a baby won't stop me from reaching my goals and I can finish school even though I will have a child. As hard as it's going to be, I've decided to keep the baby," she said, wiping the tears from my face.

My daddy is pretty upset with me, but he agrees with mama and they both agreed that I had their full support. Monty, it's not that I don't want to have a baby by you. It's the simple fact that you hurt me so badly. This baby will keep you in my life for the next eighteen years and I don't even like to be around you most days."

I pulled in the parking lot of the restaurant and found a spot. Throwing the truck in park, I turned my body around so I had direct eye contact with her. The pain on her face fucked with me in every way imaginable. Hurting her was not something I was trying to do intentionally, but it happened and I regret that shit.

"Poe, I've apologized for my actions over and over again. Mena is a thing of the past and I haven't talked to her since the incident in Chicago. I will love you even if you never take me back as your man. I was the one who fucked up what we had. The blame lies solely on me. This baby is something that we made from the love that we shared with one another. I know it may sound like bullshit, but it's not.

You are the only woman that I love. Mena wasn't shit to me. I was raised without my father, Poe. I don't want my child to live that type of life."

"Can we go inside and eat? I'm hungry," she said, avoiding what I said.

"I'm going to go in and get our food to go. We have a lot to discuss and I think we should do it in private." She opened her mouth to say something and I shook my head no. "Please don't fight me on this. It needs to be out in the open in order for us to even be able to co-parent. Okay?" She nodded yes and I got out the truck and took the keys with me. I didn't need her ass to hop in the driver's seat and leave a nigga.

***

It took about thirty minutes for our order to be ready. I ordered crab legs, jumbo shrimp, lobster, fries, and coleslaw. When I came back out, Poe was looking down at her phone. Placing the bags in the backseat, I opened the door and got in. She didn't bother to look my way and that tugged at my heart a little bit because she used to light up any time I was in her presence. Now it was like I didn't exist in her world.

Driving to my apartment, it was quiet. I reached over and turned on the radio because I wasn't going to try to force her to talk. Fifteen minutes later, we were getting out and Poetry didn't wait for me to come around to open her door. She waited for me to grab the bags and I led the way to the stairs. I unlocked the door and allowed her to enter first.

"This is a nice place. How many bedrooms do you have?" she asked.

"There's two bedrooms," I said, placing the food on the table in the kitchen.

Poetry took it upon herself to roam around my crib. She was looking in every nook and cranny to see if another bitch had been in my shit. I followed behind her slowly as she opened the door to the room that used to belong to Dray. Walking inside she continued to glance around.

"This is Dray's room, huh?"

"It was Dray's room. His ass no longer lives here. I put his ass out the day he put his hands on you. What you thought I was playing when I said that shit? He's lucky all he got was his ass whooped and put the fuck out. Come on so you can feed my baby," I said, grabbing her by the arm.

"Wait a minute. Show me your room," she said with a sly grin.

Shaking my head, I walked to my bedroom and she followed. I opened the door and ushered her in. I didn't have shit to hide, so I left her ass to play inspector gadget by her damn self. As I placed food on plates, Poetry came back in the kitchen and sat down.

"Did you find what you were looking for?" I asked, popping a fry in my mouth.

"I wasn't looking for shit, so what are you talking about?"

"It's okay. All women do what you just did. All you had to do was ask if any bitches been in my shit. You didn't have to walk through trying to see if anything was left behind," I said, laughing.

"I'm not worried about who you have in here. This yo' place and we ain't even together, so that's not my concern," she said, rolling her eyes.

I knew her ass was lying, but I didn't push it further. Sliding a plate of food to her, I sat down across from her so I would have a clear view of her pretty ass. She didn't waste no time going in on the lobster. A stream of butter ran down the corner of her mouth to her chin. I reached out without thinking and rubbed it away with my thumb.

"Thank you," she said as she continued to eat.

"How have you been?" I asked, biting into a shrimp.

"I've been okay. This morning sickness is taking a toll on me. I can barely keep my eyes open in class. No matter what time I go to bed, I'm always sleepy."

"Is there anything you need me to do?"

"Monty, all I want you to do is be there for this baby. I'm not your concern right now. I'm almost three months pregnant and I'm barely showing. Ask me that same question in seven months. Until then, I'm fine."

"I'm not about to sit around and do nothing. I'm not a deadbeat ass nigga. I've been there for you even though you can't stand my ass, it won't stop now. So, trying to push me to the back of the line about our baby is not going to work. Being here for you throughout this whole pregnancy is what I plan to do. It won't be too hard for you to keep me in the loop of your doctor's visits because I want to know about every one of them."

"You have school and whatever else you have going on to worry about. I can handle going to my appointments alone. Kaymee will go with me," she said, grabbing another piece of lobster.

Poetry was pissing me off with the quick comebacks she kept throwing at me. The only thing I wanted to do was be there for this entire experience. I didn't want to miss out on anything.

"Look, there is nothing in this world that will stop me from seeing my baby grow inside of you. I will be there to cater to your every need. Get irritated now because I will be there. So stop making excuses and go with the flow, love."

"Have you talked to Kaymee?"

"Don't try to change the subject. I don't want to talk about Mee. What I'm trying to do is get on one accord with you. This shit is important, Poe! Stop playing me like I'm a punk ass muthafucka!"

"I don't need you to be there for me! When the baby comes, we will work out some type of arrangement. Now, leave it alone!"

"Okay, fine. I'll do this shit your way—for now," I said, standing up.

I started clearing the table and Poe went into Dray's old room and closed the door. Putting the rest of the food in the refrigerator and washed the dishes, I walked to the door and knocked. Poetry didn't respond, so I knocked again. When she didn't answer the second time, I walked in. She was lying on the bed sleeping soundly and all I could do was stare at her. This was my fault. I had to fix this shit and I needed to fix it fast.

Chapter 12
Drayton

"Thank you for coming to bail me out, Melody. Take me to my apartment so I can pay you back. Then I need you to take me to get my car from that damn dorm. She better hoped my shit didn't get towed. All the shit I've done for her and this is how she repay me! Fuck that bitch!"

I spent the entire weekend in the muthafuckin' county jail behind that stupid ass bitch Kaymee. Calling and texting her ass for weeks without getting a response was the reason I showed up at her door. All she had to do was open the fuckin' door and she couldn't even do that right. Then she called security on my black ass and she would regret it. When I said there wasn't no breaking up, I meant that shit!

"Dray, I told you to tell her about the baby. This is on you because she shouldn't have found out the way she did. Honesty is the best policy and you didn't give her any reason to trust you from this point. In my opinion, you don't have the right to be upset."

"I didn't ask for your opinion, Melody! But if she wants to be with me, she has to accept all of me and that includes my child!"

"She made it clear she wasn't about to be bothered with a child that wasn't hers! She's done with you, Dray. Leave that girl alone. I don't see anything good coming from you constantly trying to get her to see things your way. Leave it alone," Melody said, walking to her car.

Other than giving Melody directions to my place, the car was eerily quiet. When we got to my apartment, I got out of her car, but she didn't. I stood waiting and she continued to sit, staring straight ahead. Sighing heavily, I walked to the driver's side and tapped on the window.

"What, Dray?"

"Get out and come up so I can repay you."

"I can sit here until you come back. We still need to go get your car and I have to be at work in an hour. You're wasting time," she snapped.

I wanted to say something back to her, but I didn't have time for her temper tantrums. Pulling my phone from my pocket, I walked into the building as I pulled up Kaymee's social media account. I went straight to her messenger as I waited for the elevator. My thumbs hoovered over the screen and I decided to back out of the app.

I went into my apartment and went straight to the safe in my closet. Keying in the code, I opened it and counted out five hundred dollars for Melody. With every move I made, Kaymee entered my mind. Her beautiful caramel skin, the way her locs framed her face, her laugh, her smile, the tears that cascaded down her face, the fear in her eyes. The fucked up part is my dick only got hard with the thought of her being scared of me.

Kaymee had another thing coming if she thought I was going to walk away and let her be with another nigga. She was mine until I said otherwise. Going back to her messenger, I left her a message.

Dray Montgomery: It was fucked up how you let me get locked up behind yo' bullshit. Take me off the block list so we can talk.

I waited a couple minutes and I saw that she read the message but didn't reply. That only made me madder. I gave her a chance to respond, but after waiting ten minutes she still hadn't responded. My blood was boiling because she was outright ignoring me.

Drayton Montgomery: You can read the message but not respond, huh? This is not what you want, Kaymee! You belong to me! I molded that pussy to fit one dick, mine! You can block me from calling and texting, but you won't be able to block my fist from going upside yo' muthfuckin' head! Keep yo' eyes open, baby. I love you.

Leaving out of my apartment, I took the stairs instead of waiting for the elevator. I was anxious to get my car. Kaymee's young ass had me acting like a fuckin' maniac over her. She was going to learn to listen or get fucked up. I knew eventually she would get her punk ass daddy involved, but I wasn't worried.

When I stepped out the door, I didn't see Melody's car. "I know her ass didn't leave," I said to myself. Taking my phone out to call her, I heard the sound of a horn blowing. I looked around and saw her flashing her lights. I calmed myself down and trotted over to where she was parked. Getting in, I could tell she was irritated.

"What took you so long? I thought I told you that I had to be at work!"

"Lower your voice when you to talk to me, Mel. I'm not trying to hear yo' shit right now," I said, handing her the money.

She took the money and threw it in her purse before peeling out of the spot. She drove fast as hell all the way to Kaymee's dorm. When we got there, I didn't see my car and that only ignited my anger.

"Where the fuck is my car?"

"I don't know, Dray. You are going to have to figure that out on your own. I have to get to work. I'm not missing out on money because you were over here on bullshit. Find your car and leave that girl alone."

"I will pay you for the day. I need to get my car, Mel!"

"I have an important meeting and I can't miss it. I'm sorry. I gotta go," she said, unlocking the doors.

"So, you just gon' turn yo' back on me?"

"It's not about turning my back on you! I have a damn clock to punch in order for me to eat! I don't have easy money falling in my lap! I work hard for my shit! You ain't never known me to sit around waiting for a muthafucka to do nothing for me. So, you can keep that reverse psychology shit for them young bitches that you have wrapped around your finger. Get out of my car, Dray!"

"Who the fuck do you think you're talking to, Mel? I will—"

"You'll what? Open your eyes so you can see who you're talking to. If you're thinking about putting your hands on me, I will blow your fuckin' head off. I don't play the hitting game with anybody. Those other hoes may let you use them as punching bags, but that shit won't fly over here. Now, for the last time, get out of my fuckin' car!"

Melody had never raised her voice to me. On the other hand, I had never talked reckless to her either. But because she was pregnant with my child, I was going to let her slide with that slick ass shit that rolled off her tongue. I didn't need her to take me nowhere. I'd get an Uber. Opening the door, I placed my foot on the ground and paused. I turned my head and stared at her for what felt like an eternity.

"You got one mo' time to talk to me like that. Trust me when I tell you, the outcome won't be the same next time. Your little threats don't move me and neither do your brothers. I have never put my hands on yo' ass, but shit like that would give me the green light to choke the fuck outta you. Don't start worrying about these birdbrain bitches. The way I treat you should be the only thing that matters," I said, getting out of the car slamming the door.

Melody drove off like she was driving in an *Indy 500* race. I didn't care if she was in her feelings. She would be calling talking about, 'baby daddy, I'm hungry' or some silly shit like that. I watched the back of her car until she rounded the corner.

I pulled my phone off my hip and went to the Uber app to summon a ride when I thought about Alexis. Usually I would call Monty for shit like this but, he's been acting like a hoe ass nigga. I dialed her number and the phone didn't even ring fully before she picked up.

"Where have you been, Dray? I've been calling you since Friday—"

"Shut up and come pick me up from Abby Hall!" I said, cutting her ass off. I didn't have time for her mouth after the shit I had to listen to with Melody.

"Abby Hall? What the fuck you doing over there? Oh, you're there with that bitch, ain't you? I'm not coming to get you! Tell that bitch to take you where you need to go!"

"Yo' ass bet not hang up that muthafuckin' phone!" I yelled before she could disconnect. She knew what was up because I heard her breathing heavily. "I need you to give me a ride to the pound so I can get my car. I've been locked up since Friday and your smart mouth is something I don't want to hear right now," I said through clenched teeth.

"You don't have to lie, Dray. I'm on my way because you fuckin' me after this shit!" she said, hanging up on me.

I laughed out loud because I couldn't believe how these females were coming at me. An alert chimed from my phone and I looked down at it. There was a messenger notification letting me know Kaymee responded to the message I sent. Rushing to open it, I began to read.

Sassylocs: My bullshit? That was all you, boo. I didn't invite you to my place and I damn sure didn't tell you to act a fool with the police. The only thing you have to do is leave me the fuck alone. Another thing, I hope you remember what this pussy feels like because you will never get the chance to crawl between my legs again. You must've forgotten who my daddy was. Don't threaten me about what you're gonna do to me because you will die, Dray. I know you are expecting me to block you, but I won't. Stay away from me if you value your life.

This bitch was out of her mind! Kaymee thought I was playing with her. I was going to have to show her that I wasn't. She was going to get the surprise of her life as soon as I felt the time was right to pay her a visit. I had to let time pass because she was ready for me to show up.

Chapter 13
Poetry

As I sat in my Psychology class, it was hard to concentrate on what the professor was saying because my head was pounding. The back of my eyes was killing me and I could barely see. I never heard of anyone saying they had major headaches during their pregnancy. It was an everyday occurrence along with morning sickness. I didn't know how much more I could take.

"I want you guys to study chapters thirteen through twenty because there will be a test on. It will be multiple choice as well as essay. This test will be a major part of your midterm grade, so make it count," the professor said.

It was the middle of October and I was four and a half months pregnant. Monty had been coming over to check on me even though I'd told him not to. My stomach was getting rounder and he didn't miss a beat rubbing my baby bump. As hard as I tried to stay mad at him, I couldn't. He was evolving into a responsible man right before my eyes. Getting back with him was still something I wasn't going to do, but we were learning to be friends.

"Poetry, are you planning on staying here for the rest of the morning?" the professor asked.

Looking around the classroom, I noticed that class had been dismissed. "No, I'm sorry. I didn't realize class was over. I've been battling a severe headache all morning. I did hear you say we were having a test on chapters thirteen through twenty. I'll be ready," I said, placing my book in my backpack. Wednesday

"If you need a couple days out of class, I can set it up to where you can follow along online. I know how hard it is to be pregnant and attend school. Your energy level isn't what it used to be. I've done it three times myself," my professor said, chuckling.

"No, I'm fine for the moment. If things change, I will surely take you up on that offer. Thank you for understanding and I'll see you on Wednesday."

"Take care, Poetry," she called out as I left out of her class.

My eleven o'clock class was cancelled because the professor was out sick. I was relieved because I could go back to my dorm and sleep. Stepping out the building, the sunlight blinded me and my head started pounding. It sounded like a set of drums were beating deep in my ear canal. I pressed hard on the bridge of my nose. That usually helped, but it did nothing for me that day.

I rested my head on the wall and closed my eyes. The pain was one I couldn't describe. I just knew it hurt like hell and my vision was blurred. Turning my head away from the sun, I blinked a couple times, but it didn't help. I felt a hand rubbing my back and I glanced over my shoulder. Montez was staring at me with a worried look in his eyes.

"Are you alright, Poe?" I couldn't do anything other than shake my head no. "You're having headaches again?"

"Yes, this time I can barely see. I think my blood pressure may be elevated. I had a sausage, egg and cheese croissant from Burger King this morning. The sausage is probably what caused my headache. I will check my pressure when I get back to the dorm," I said, squinting to see his face.

"Poe, you're going to have to stop eating all that bullshit. I will make it my business to bring you home cooked breakfast every morning. We have to change your diet because I can't stomach seeing you suffering," he said, massaging my temple.

His touch was easing the pain and I couldn't swat his hand away like my mind was demanding me to do. Monty was right, I needed to change my eating habits and fast. I just didn't want him catering to me like I was his woman.

"You don't have to do that. I'll make sure I eat less salt."

"I know I don't have to do it, Poe. It's something I want to do for you and the baby. Come on so I can take you home. I'll come back to get your car later," he said taking hold of my arm.

"Why are you here anyway, Monty?" I asked, laying my head on his arm. He put his arm around my waist and locked his right hand with mine.

"I came to see you before your next class and happened to see you about ready to pass out."

Monty helped me into the passenger seat of his car and it felt good to be able to rest and close my eyes. I was out like a light before he even pulled off. At least I think I was. My dorm was on the other side of the building and it wouldn't be long before I was inside sleeping in my bed.

I woke up after some time and I was in bed and under the covers. It only meant Monty didn't worry about waking me. He brought me inside and made sure I was comfortable. Swinging my legs out of bed, my head was still hurting but not as much. I got up slowly and followed Kaymee's voice.

"I've been concentrating on school. I haven't been communicating with you purposely," I heard her saying.

"That's understandable. You already know how I am about you and Poe. Making sure y'all straight is what I do. Atlanta is like Chicago and I want y'all to be careful. Don't let this campus fool you. Outside of these walls is still the ghetto, remember that," Monty said.

What was he still doing here? I looked down at my watch and it was damn near three o'clock in the afternoon. My vision became hazy a little bit and I leaned against the wall and closed my eyes. When I looked up, both of them were staring at me.

"Yo' head still hurting Poe?" Monty asked as he stood up and walked toward me.

"Yeah, a little bit. I have to check my pressure."

"I checked it when we got in and it was a little high. I went out and got you a turkey wrap and a salad. Would you consider drinking more water than pop and juice, please?"

Monty wasn't about to be trying to regulate what I did with myself. If I wasn't trying to harm myself, then he shouldn't have anything to say. Ignoring him, I went to the refrigerator and grabbed the food he bought as well as a bottled water. I noticed he also bought a lot of fruit that he knew I liked and breakfast food.

"Thank you, but I don't need you to treat me like a child. I'm capable of taking care of myself, Montez," I said, turning to Kaymee. "Hey, sis. How you been? I miss you even though we live in the same dorm," I said, unwrapping my food as I sat down.

"I've been doing good. We are halfway through the semester and I'm glad. These classes have been kicking my ass, but I'm on top of them all. Enough about me. How has Teetee's baby been treating you?"

"This pregnancy is giving me hell! I'm almost five months and I'm forever throwing up. I have morning, noon, and night sickness almost every day. I've tried crackers and ginger ale and it's not working,"

"It will get better for you, sis. How are classes coming along?"

"I'm doing pretty well even though I can barely stay awake during my morning classes. I found out this morning that I can attend class online if I need to. Once I get further along in this pregnancy, that's probably what I'm going to have to consider," I said, taking a bite of the wrap.

Monty cleared his throat and I glanced at him across the table. It was a shame how he could still make my lady parts moist without touching me. His hair was freshly cut and I could smell his cologne from where I was sitting.

"When is your next doctor's appointment, Poe? I have yet to attend one," Monty asked.

"The appointment is the first week of next month. Kaymee has been going with me, so you don't have to."

"I have?" Kaymee asked confused.

"Yes!" I sneered at her.

"Ummm, okay," she said, still trying to figure out what I was doing.

"Well Kaymee, you don't have to go anymore because I'll be taking her from now on. Poetry, I need you to keep me in the loop of all your appointments. There are many questions that I need answers to and I want to be there to ask the doctor."

"Tell me what you want to know and I'll ask. I want Kaymee to be there with me. You don't have to come. We are not about to argue over this, Montez."

"I know we're not about to argue. It's not that deep, ma. Kaymee didn't help you produce this baby. I did that. Being there every step of the way is important to me, Poe. I've already missed the one last month and I don't plan to miss anymore."

Kaymee's phone chiming back to back interrupting the spat Monty and I were having. "Who the hell is trying to get your attention so tough?" I asked.

"Girl, it's Dray. I blocked him from my phone, so his only way to get in touch with me is through messenger. He has been getting on my damn nerves, but I've been ignoring him. Since the day I got my cast off, there hasn't been much to say to his ass."

"I didn't even notice your cast was off. When did that happen and what the hell happened with Dray?" Monty asked, resting his arm on the table.

"I got it taken off a couple weeks ago and I saw Dray and his baby mama in the hospital cafeteria. I'm done with him Monty, so you don't have to worry about anything. I got this."

"Well if that nigga tries to do anything to you, I want you to let me know."

Monty was ready to kick Dray's ass and I was all for it. Kaymee didn't tell him about Dray acting a damn fool and going to jail. It wasn't my place to say anything, so I sat and ate my food. I'm glad his attention was on her and not me because I was getting tired of him hounding me.

"Dray isn't going to do anything stupid. He needs to concentrate on being a daddy and leave me the hell alone. I have more important shit to worry about."

"Don't wait until the last minute to call me if he gets outta his body," Monty said, standing up. "I'll be back tonight around seven to take you to dinner, Poe. Be ready," he said, kissing my cheek.

"I don't want to—"

"Did I ask you what you wanted to do? I want to take the mother of my child out to dinner. Can I do that, please? Wear something nice, too. See you later, Kaymee," he said, winking at me as he left.

Picking at my salad, I thought about how hard Monty was trying to do right by me. He was doing everything right, but I didn't know if I could trust him to be with only me. My feelings for him hadn't waivered and I didn't want him to think it was going to be more than us being just friends. Yes, we made a baby, but we would never be together again.

"Poetry, Monty loves you and I can see his efforts at proving it that are being swept under the rug. He messed up and I think he is truly sorry. Give him a chance to make things right. Some guys don't give a damn about their baby mamas, but Monty is trying to be there for you during your pregnancy and you are pushing him to the side."

"Mee, I don't want him to believe I want to get back with him. That will never happen. As much as I love him, he hurt me. There's nothing he can do to right his wrong," I said as her phone dinged again. "Is that Dray again?"

"Yeah, I didn't want to open the messages while Monty was here. Poetry, I'm going to tell you something but promise not to tell Monty," she said nervously.

"Kaymee, what's going on? I'm not promising anything until I know what I'm not supposed to tell him."

She opened the messenger on her phone and slid it to me. When I opened the messages, my mouth hit the floor. This fool was crazy. I started reading the messages she hadn't took the liberty to look at out loud.

Drayton Montgomery: So you gon' just keep ignoring me, right?

Drayton Montgomery: I know you read every mutha-fuckin' message!

Drayton Montgomery: You owe me $600 for my car get-ting impounded, bitch!

Drayton Montgomery: Kaymee, you belong to me! If I see you with another nigga, his ass is dead!

Drayton Montgomery: I'm gon' beat yo' ass when I see you!

Drayton Montgomery: I'm sorry, Kaymee, I didn't mean none of the shit I said. I love you. Can we go out and talk? I miss you, baby.

As I was reading the last message, another one came through.

Drayton Montgomery: I see you online and you still ain't responding! Make me fuck you up!

"And I'm supposed to keep quiet about this? Nah, you have to tell Monty or Jonathan. Dray sounds like a fuckin' lunatic, sis. Look back at how he acted when he came here banging on the door! Kaymee, we have to say something before he does something bad to you!"

"Poe, he won't do anything to me. I haven't been responding to him. Dray will eventually go away. He has plenty of other females to entertain."

"But he wants you! I don't see him going away quietly, Kaymee. You are taking this too lightly. Something is terribly wrong with this nigga and it will be a matter of time before he acts on his threats. I don't want it to come to that. He is basically stalking you! Don't erase none of these messages. As a matter of fact, screenshot all of them and send them to my phone! Anything else he sends, I want those, too. Be careful with this nigga, Kaymee. I won't say nothing right now, but the minute you stop forwarding messages, I'm going straight to Jonathan."

"You'd have every right to do that if I stop communicating. I'm not worried about, Dray."

I didn't like the way she was being so nonchalant about the whole thing. She probably wasn't taking his ass seriously, but I knew all about men that didn't want to let go. Shit could get dangerous really quick. According to the shit he said, he was getting fed up with her not giving him the attention he was seeking.

"This shit just spoiled my appetite," I said with a bad taste in my mouth.

Before I could finish wrapping my food, I felt bile creeping into my throat. Jumping up from the table, I raced to the bathroom, barely making it to the toilet. Everything I had eaten was now spurting out of my mouth. Throwing up was part of my daily routine and I hated it.

Kaymee came in and pulled my hair back from my face. "Here, drink this," she said, holding out a bottled water.

When I raised my head, I had to bury it back into the bowl. It felt like I was throwing up a lung. I wasn't built for this thing called pregnancy. It was lowkey trying to take me out. Nothing else was coming up after about five minutes and all I could do was dry heave. Standing to my feet, I went to the sink and rinsed my mouth before I put toothpaste on my toothbrush.

"Drink this first, Poe. If you're throwing up like this all the time, you may want to buy some Gatorade to stay hydrated. Monty already bought a couple cases of water, so you're good there," Kaymee said, handing me the water.

"I'm going to have to ask the doctor about this because I don't think I'm supposed to be sick all day," I said after taking a couple sips of the water. "Let me brush my teeth, then I'll lay down. I don't have anymore classes today."

"I have to go to class at five but I will be back. Rest up so you will feel better to go out with my brother," she said with a smile.

"That's not going to happen. I don't feel good."

"You're using this as an excuse. Your ass is going! Stop treating him like that. He has suffered enough," Kaymee said with her hand on her hip.

"Whatever. Your brother caused all of this ruckus. Don't forget that part," I said, sticking the toothbrush in my mouth.

"Well, he said he's sorry!" she whined.

Spitting in the sink, I looked at her through the mirror, "Dray did too after he threatened you in the same breath. I'm not trying to hear that shit, Kaymee."

"Dray is not Monty! We have known him forever, Poe!"

"I thought I knew him, but I guess I was wrong. I don't know him at all," I said, rinsing my mouth and walking out.

Listening to Kaymee defend Montez pissed me off. She would never understand the level of hurt I was going through behind him. My mind was made up. Fuck Montez. I made it to my room and closed the door. That was an indication for her not to follow me because the conversation was over.

Chapter 14
Kaymee

I decided to take a nap after Poetry went in her room and closed the door. The chime of my phone prevented me from sleeping and I was irritated to the max. Poetry was right about Dray because he was blowing my phone up. Scared was an understatement, I was terrified. Giving him the satisfaction of knowing he put fear in me was something I would try my best to keep hidden.

Picking up the phone, I had twenty-five messages sitting in my inbox. It was four o'clock and I wanted to grab me a caramel Frappuccino to keep me awake long enough to get me through my four hour class. As I put on my shoes, three more messages were sent to me. It was time for me to block Dray's ass but I knew once I did that, he was going to start following me.

My backpack was sitting in the chair by the window. I walked over and switched books, making sure I had everything I would need for class. Pulling my door closed, I went to Poetry's room to check on her before I headed out. She was laying on her side breathing lightly with her hand resting on her little belly. I smiled as I closed the door because I was so excited for her and Monty. The baby will bring them closer together the way it should've been anyway.

With my car keys in hand as I exited the building, my eyes swept the parking lot before I descended the stairs. Dray had me on pins and needles because I didn't know what he was bound to do. Even though he hadn't been back since the night I called security, I knew he was mad about getting locked up.

Relief was what I felt when I sat inside the car without any incidents occurring. I pressed the push start button and put my seat belt on. When I put my car in reverse, my phone started ringing and I answered without looking at the screen. I continued backing up before I said anything.

"Hello."

"That car fits you, Miss Morrison. That's how you been getting by me. I've been waiting for you to walk up, not realizing daddy bought you a new whip. Now that I know what you're driving, the next time you ignore me, you may end up in a ditch because your brakes went out," Dray said lowly. "Stop playing with me because I can make your life a living hell."

"How far do you think you're going to get by forcing your way into my life? I won't be pressured into being with you, Dray. The time we spent together was great until you fucked it up. Please understand that we are done. I don't want to put a restraining order on you, but I will."

"It's just a piece of paper, idiot! The police would have to make it to yo' ass in order to save you. I told you before, it's not over until I say it's over!"

I couldn't stop the laugh that escaped my mouth, "You have one ghetto ass bitch and a baby mama that I know of. There's no telling how many others are out there claiming to have rode your dick. This drama is something I want no parts of. Go play with the bitches that you have because I'm on to bigger and better things. There isn't a time slot with your name on it anywhere in my life. This is the way you wanted it obviously when you changed on me. It's over, Dray. Live with it," I said, hanging up before he could reply.

At that point, I didn't want to go to Starbucks. Shit, I wanted to skip class altogether. My nerves were all over the place because I didn't know what Dray was going to try to pull. I kept glancing in the rearview mirror but each time, there was no sign of his crazy ass and I was sort of relieved.

As I cruised down the street, out of nowhere, there was a hard bump to the back of my car. Fighting not to swerve in the next lane, I tried to see who was in the car behind me. There was no way I could stop to make the turn into the campus parking lot, so I was forced to keep going. After hanging up on Dray, I threw my phone into the passenger seat and it was out of reach.

I kept going straight down Spelman Lane Southwest and cut a right, barely missing the curb. Hitting another right at the next corner, I was literally speeding down Spelman Lane. Getting to the campus police department was the task I was trying to complete.

As I got to Westview Drive Southwest, the car was still behind me picking up speed. My car was hit again, but this time from the left side and I almost lost control and ran into a mailbox. Avoiding a collision, I turned right and pushed the gas pedal, pushing the car up the street. I glanced in the rearview mirror and the car was no longer behind me, but I continued toward the police station anyway.

I didn't have a choice but to put in a report. My father would go crazy from the damage done to the car let alone Dray trying to run me off the road. I didn't have to see his face to know it was him. He was really trying to hurt me because I didn't want to be bothered with him anymore. Why did shit always have to happen to me? All I wanted was to be happy for once in my life.

Parking in front of the police station, I jumped out of the car and ran inside. The officer at the desk was shuffling through some papers and looked up as I entered. The expression on my face must've had fear written on it because he stood immediately.

"Is everything okay, ma'am?"

Finding my voice was hard because I couldn't stop shaking. "I was just in a road rage altercation. My car was rammed from the back and the driver also tried to force me off the road from the side. I don't know what I could've done. I was on my way to class," my voice quaked with every word I spoke.

"Did you get a look at the vehicle or the driver?" the officer asked.

"No, I was trying to concentrate on getting to a safe location. I remembered there was a police station close by and headed for it. All I know is the car was beat up and it was grey."

"Okay, you stay here while I go out and look at the damage done to your car," he said, rounding the counter.

I sat in a nearby chair and reached for my phone, but I had left it in the car. Standing, I went to the door and peeked out. The officer was looking at the back of my car writing on a pad. He walked to the driver's side and started writing again.

"Would you please bring my purse and phone to me?" I asked as he was coming back toward the door.

He doubled back and grabbed my belongings and handed them to me as I held the door open for him. "The damage isn't too bad, but they did hit you pretty good in the rear. I will get a report together so you can take it to your insurance company. Some people don't need to drive if little things will make them do something like this over nothing. I'm going to need your license to complete the report. I'll have you out of here soon. Sit tight."

Calling Jonathan was the last thing I wanted to do because he was going to have so many questions. Lying to the police was easy, but it was going to be hard to do the same to my daddy because he was going to see right through it. He had all the insurance information and it was going to be hard to hide the damage. It would be better to tell him about it now rather than later.

I was scared to make the call, but I did. I listened to the phone ringing and when he answered, I could here Katrina giggling in the background. "It's Kaymee. I have to see if everything is okay," he said, moving around. It took a minute before he actually gave me his undivided attention. "Hey, baby girl. What's up?"

"Someone hit the car and I'm at the campus police station,"

"Are you hurt?" he asked, getting serious.

"No, I'm not hurt. A little shook up, but fine."

"What happened, Kaymee?"

I hesitated for a minute before I answered. "I was driving to class and a car rammed the back of my car. Then I was almost forced off the road from the driver's side," I said as tears burned my eyes.

"Do you know who was in the muthafucka was in the car?" he asked with a lot of venom behind it.

"What's going on, bae?" I heard Katrina ask.

"Hold on, Trina. I'll fill you in when I get off the phone," he said, silencing her. "I need to know what kind of car it was and what they looked like." His voice boomed through the phone and I knew then, he was beyond pissed.

"Daddy, all I know is the car was raggedy and beat up. I didn't see who was driving."

"I'm on my way. Don't move. As a matter of fact, I will call Monty to come sit with you until I get there. Make sure you get a police report. I'll see you soon, baby girl," he said, hanging up.

I was silently praying Dray went about his business because he was going to die if he showed up. My phone started ringing in my hand and Monty's name popped up on the screen. I didn't want to answer, but I had to so he didn't think anything else happened.

"Hey, bro."

"You good? I'm about five minutes away and had to hear your voice for myself. Did Dray do this shit, Kaymee?"

"Like I told my daddy, I don't know who it was, Monty." The pitch of my voice went up a couple of octaves and I was getting frustrated.

"I'm pulling up now and this conversation is not over," he said, disconnecting the call.

I sat wringing my fingers when my phone chimed. I looked down and I had yet another message from Dray in my messenger. To be honest, I was afraid of what he had to say this time around.

Dray Montgomery: I see you called reinforcement. You better hope them niggas don't come for me because yo' ass will come up missin'. Keep your mouth closed, Kaymee.

Monty was walking around my car when I glanced out the window. The grimace on his face was one that said murder without words. His lips were together so tightly, they were changing colors. Marching to the entrance of the police station, he snatched the door open and stood glaring at me.

"Mee, come outside for a minute." I got up and walked out of the door he was holding open for me. Once we got by my car, he folded his arms over his chest. "I'm gon' ask you one more time. Did Dray do this shit?"

"No, Monty! I don't know who did it, okay!" I said, looking down playing with my fingers.

"Why are you protecting this nigga? He could've killed you!" he yelled with fire in his eyes. "I know you better than you know yourself, especially when you are trying to keep something from me."

"I don't know who it was in that car! The only thing I want to do is get my car to the shop and go on with my life. If I knew who it was, I would tell you. It was a case of road rage. That's all I can think of because I don't know anyone here!"

"Yeah a'ight. Keep the lie going," he said as a tow truck bulled up in front of my car.

Jonathan's Benz came to a stop behind my car and he jumped out with Katrina right behind him. My daddy came up to me and wrapped his arms around my waist before he checked every part of my body to make sure I was alright. I could tell he thought I was harmed in some way before he laid eyes on me. Even though I had already told him I was fine.

"If I find out who did this shit, I'm going back to jail. There will be no pity on the muthafucka at all. In the back of my mind, I think Dray has something to do with this. You told me that y'all was through. Was it his choice or yours?" he asked, looking down on me.

"It was my choice, but I don't think he had anything to do with this."

"You sure about that?" Monty asked sarcastically.

"Don't you have a date to get ready for?" I asked, rolling my eyes. "To answer your question, yes, I am sure. The car that hit me is one I've never seen before. I know what Dray's car looks like."

"That don't mean the nigga didn't do the shit, Kaymee," Monty continued to probe. "It don't matter because I'm gon' go pay that nigga a visit anyway."

"Has he been harassing you, Kaymee? If he has, I'll put my foot in his ass for that alone," Jonathan said angrily.

"No! Would the two of you just stop pointing fingers please! Damn, hurting people is what y'all live for and would use anything to do it! Just take me to my dorm, somebody!"

"I'll take you because I'm going there to pick up Poe," Monty said as he pushed the remote start button to start his car.

"Daddy, here are my keys. I'm about to go inside and see if the report is ready, then I'm leaving."

Not waiting for him to respond, I stomped inside the police station. "Everything is ready for you, Miss Morrison. I hope everything goes well for you," the officer said, handing me the report and my license.

"Thank you for all of your help," I responded and turned to walk out the door.

When I stepped out, I saw Dray standing on the other side of the parking lot, leaned against a tree. Jonathan and Monty were talking, so it seemed I was the only one that saw him. He was waving at me and laughing. Then I saw him pull out his phone and walked out of sight. It wasn't long before my phone vibrated in my purse. I would check the message later when no one was around.

"Monty, I'm ready."

I handed my daddy the report, kissed his cheek, and gave Katrina a hug before walking to Monty's car. I sat thinking about how much more shit I was going to have to go through with Dray before he got the picture to leave me alone.

Chapter 15
Drayton

I know it was wrong for me to try to run Kaymee off the road, but I told her not to play with me. When she sped towards that mailbox, I knew she was about to wreck her shit and hit it head on. I was beating the steering wheel when she swerved and missed that muthafucka. She got one up on me when I noticed she was heading for the police station. Backing up off of her was my only option because I want' trying to roll behind her and end up back behind bars.

Standing in the cut watching her every move, I was waiting for another opportunity to attack. Monty ass pulled up and I knew trying to run her off the road was all the fun I would have that day. It was far from over though because I was just beginning. Kaymee saw me across the lot and her reaction was priceless. She was bothered just like I wanted her to be. But she didn't snitch on me because them niggas didn't try to do anything. Shit, I don't think she even said anything to bring attention my way.

I left and got in my car and drove to the crib. There were a couple cats that wanted Xanax and Molly, so I was about to hit them up and make this money. As I stepped through the door, my phone started ringing. I pulled it from my hip and Alexis was calling.

"Yo, I got some business to handle. I'll hit you when I'm on my way back to the crib so you can come over and swallow this dick."

"Is that all you care about? I was just trying to call to see how you were doing," she shot back with attitude.

"Alexis, you know I'm not trying to hear shit other than how you want me to suck it. All that other shit you can keep. What's it gon' be? Are you coming through or do I need to take an alternate route? It's all on you, baby," I said, packing up the pills I needed for my run.

"I'll be there, but you are going to stop treating me like a fuckin' hoe, Dray!"

"I treat yo' ass how you loved to be treated in the beginning. Ain't shit changed. The only difference is you get to cuddle a little longer than before. Other than that, it's the same shit. Ain't no love between us, so leave that shit outside when you come to my shit. I gotta go, but I'll hit you up when I'm ready for you."

Hitting the end button, I packed up six hundred dollars' worth of Molly and a grand of Xanax. These privileged ass college boys were trying to party like rock stars, but I wasn't one to tell them not to. Shit, they were putting bread in my pocket and I was loving the shit. Printing out the labels for the bottles, I placed them on the correct ones and put them in my pocket.

Protecting myself in case I got stopped by the law was a must. I took that shit off before I made the sale, though. I left out and took the stairs because I didn't have time to wait on the elevator. I wanted to get in this car and drive my ass off.

Picking up my phone, I hit up the dude I was bringing the pills to. I hoped his ass was at the meeting spot because I was not trying to be sitting around. His ass drove over an hour to cop from me, coming from the University of Georgia all the way to Atlanta to get high.

"Yeah, Sam. I'm here waiting for you."

"A'ight, bet. It's the usual sixteen hunnid. Have my shit ready so I can roll out."

Hanging up, I dropped the phone between my legs and hit the button to turn on the radio. R Kelly's "When a Woman's Fed up" came on. I reached over to turn it off, but

I my finger wouldn't push the button because the chorus started and I was stuck.

Cause when a woman's fed up
No matter how you beg, no
It ain't nothing you can do about it
It's like running out of love
No matter what you say, no
And then it's too late to talk about it

R Kelly didn't know shit! Kaymee wasn't going to be fed up until I gave her permission. She was going to talk to me and everything would be just like it was in Chicago. Thinking about what we were going through, I turned the radio completely off and drove the ten minutes to the club I was going to.

I parked in front and hit ole boy up to bring his ass outside. My attitude was fucked up at that point. Taking the labels off the bottles, I watched the door for him to come out. He walked his scrawny ass out and I hit the locks so he could get in.

"Thanks, Sam, for always comin' through for a nigga," he said, rubbing his hands together.

"Man, let me tell you something. I don't give a fuck how many black friends you have. If you ever let that word roll off yo' muthafuckin' lips again, I will shoot yo' ass in the mouth! Respect my culture. Now give me my money!"

"My bad—"

"Give me the money and get the fuck out!"

I was losing patience with this asshole and he wasn't moving fast enough for me. He finally gave me the money and I threw the bottles at his ass and put the gear in drive. He jumped out and I was pulling off before the door closed completely. With all the shit that were going on, I wasn't letting shit slide with these bitches that thought they could be like us.

It didn't take me long to get back to my apartment. I rolled a blunt so when I got in the crib, I could enjoy the haze. Hopping out of the car, I almost made it to the door when I heard Alexis' voice behind me.

"You ready for me, baby?" she purred in my ear.

"Alexis, what I tell you about calling me that shit?" I asked, turning around.

My eyes traveled up and down her body and I loved what I had standing in front of me. Alexis had on a light trench coat that was wide open. Underneath she had on a hunter green panty set that left nothing to the imagination. Her twins were sitting up right and her nipple rings were protruding through the material of her bra. Alexis had thighs that were thick and voluptuous as hell. I couldn't wait to get her upstairs to get between them.

"Damn, ma. That's how you coming for a nigga? That's what I'm talking about. Bring yo' sexy ass on so we can go get this party started," I said, holding the door open for her.

Alexis walked passed me and her hips swayed from left to right and I could tell the panties she had on were a thong. I could see the slit of her ass crack eating the fuck out of her coat. I was mesmerized with every step she took towards the elevator. When we got on, I attacked her mouth and my hands roamed all over her ass.

I roughly turned her to the wall and lifted her coat. Freeing my pipe, I moved the tiny string to the side with my right hand and pushed the emergency stop button with the left. Propping her leg up on the railing, I eased into her wetness and held back the groan that fought to come out of my throat.

"Shit! Just like that, baby," Alexis moaned as she pushed back on me.

Gripping her hips, I went balls deep into her pussy. I was standing on the tip of my toes because my nut was racing to the finish line. The sound of her juices mixed with our bodies connecting was music to my ears. Alexis dropped her leg and squeezed on my dick as she bent over and grabbed her ankles. That position gave me all access to get all the way in her tunnel. I felt the tip of my shit hit her G-spot over and over, then she splashed all on my tool.

"Aaaaaah! Yes, keep hitting that spot!" she screamed out as her love box released all of her sweet nectar.

I had to hold her for a few minutes while she came down from the best orgasm she'd ever had. Slapping her on the ass, she stood as I pulled the button out. The elevator started rising to my floor as I fixed myself before the elevator doors opened. There was a couple waiting to get on and I couldn't help but smile. They were going to be on some freaky shit when they saw the puddle that was left on the floor as well as the smell of sex that was bound to fill their nostrils.

Once we got inside my apartment, Alexis went straight to the bathroom while I sat at the bar. She didn't know I was about to work her ass over with my mixture of Molly and Lean with a side of haze. I had to fuck in order to keep my mind off the shit I had going on with Kaymee.

Placing the Molly under my tongue, I let it dissolve slowly. I mixed my drink and grabbed my blunt out of my pocket and put it on top of the bar. As I was removing my shirt, Alexis was coming out of the bathroom in nothing but the skin she was born in.

"Damn, you are sexy as hell, Lexi," I said, licking my lips.

I threw my shirt on the sofa and stood. Unbuckling my pants, I kicked my shoes off and let my pants fall to the floor. Alexis walked over and dropped to her knees. She tongued the tip of my dick, licking her dried up juices off. As good as it felt, I needed to smoke and drink before I had her balled up like a pretzel.

The Molly was almost gone but I wanted her to feel like me. Lifting her arm so she could stand, I stuck my tongue in her mouth. Transferring the piece of pill in her mouth, she spit it out in her hand and gave it back.

"That's all you, Dray. I don't pop pills and didn't know that you got high off your own supply. Be careful with that shit. It can destroy you. What you got to drink over here?" she asked, scanning the bottles I had lined up.

"You can have some of this lean," I said, taking a sip from the cup.

"Lean? Dray, you have changed. What's going on with you?"

"Ain't nothing going on with me. Make yo' drink and stop worrying about my recreational activities. Get that pussy right so I can beat that shit up when I'm ready for it," I said, taking a huge gulp of the liquid.

Alexis ended up pouring a hefty glass of Remy. I fired up the blunt and tried to pass it to her. Shaking her head, she went back to the bathroom and came back out with her coat and purse.

"I have my own, but thanks for the offer. Early on I was taught if I didn't see a blunt being rolled, don't smoke it," she said seriously.

"What, you don't trust me?"

"Dray, you over there drinking lean and popping Mollies, I don't know what the fuck you rolled up in that blunt besides weed. I'm good on that shit," she said as she licked the white owl sexily.

My dick thumped hard as hell because I couldn't wait for her to wrap her lips around it. Drinking the lean faster than usual, I puffed on the blunt as I kept my eyes on Alexis and her beautiful assets. The way she sucked on that blunt had a nigga thinking a bunch of nasty shit from the sight alone.

Feeling really good, I was ready to fuck. "Come here, Lexi," I said lowly.

She stubbed out her blunt and threw back the rest of the Remy in her glass. Sauntering over to where I sat, she stood between my legs. My eyes lowered to her fat pussy lips and I felt the saliva building up in my mouth. I swallowed hard and ran my hand down the crack of her ass while my other hand massage her clit.

Alexis' head fell back and the pleasure on her face was beautiful. Standing from the stool, I grabbed her hand and led her to my bedroom. Alexis eased onto the bed on her back and I crawled between her legs and devoured her clit. She instantly grabbed the back of my head and grinded her mound into my mouth.

Her clit hardened on my tongue and I wrapped my lips around it. "Ssssss, aaaaaaaahhhh! Eat that pussy," Alexis moaned, digging her nails into my shoulders. "I'm about to cum, Dray!"

Words wasn't what I wanted to respond with. I continued assaulting her clit by running my tongue over it repeatedly. Her lady parts were soaking wet just how I liked it. Sticking my tongue deep into her love cave, I stiffened it and fucked her good with only my mouth. She attempted to close her legs and I pushed them open wide with my hands.

Sucking hard on her clit, her legs starting shaking and I knew she was ready to make it rain. This was what I loved the most about Alexis, she squirted if I was eating her out or fucking her. Either way, my thirst was going to get quenched.

"Here it comes! Oh shit! Fuck!" she screamed out in ecstasy as her nectar shot down my throat.

I swallowed most of it, but I had to spit the rest out before my ass drowned. Clearing my throat, I went back to the task at hand, bringing her to another orgasm. Alexis was trying to scoot away from me, but I wouldn't let up. This was one of the reasons she was crazy as hell. I made love to her ass instead of fucking and telling her to get out.

Running my hand down my face, I used the wetness as lubricant on my dick. Her kitty was soaked and I slid right in. I pushed her legs back to her ears and fucked her hard. My mind was wandering to a place of its own and I didn't realize until it was too late.

"Oh, shit. This pussy is so good, baby. You like the way I make you feel?" I said lowly in her ear.

"Yes, daddy," she moaned back.

Her nails were digging deeper into my back with every stroke and I felt every tear. Sweat was dripping into my eyes and it stung like a muthafucka. It was an indication that the Molly and Lean was taking effect. I looked down and Kaymee's face was what I saw. A big ass smile was on my face and I slowed down my stroke.

"I love you so much, baby. This my pussy, right?"

"Yesssss, it's your pussy, Dray. It's yours, baby."

"I will kill yo' ass if you give my pussy away, Kaymee. Don't ever betray me like that."

In my head, Kaymee was the woman lying beneath me. I was making love to my woman and it felt good as hell. I picked up speed because she was not about to leave me alone. I was about to plant my seed so deep in her. She was going to have my baby and there was nothing she would be able to do about it.

"You gon' have my baby tonight, Kaymee. I'm about to cum," I said, pumping harder.

"Get the fuck off me, Dray!" she yelled.

"Naw, we are about to have a family," I moaned in her ear as I licked her lobe. "Aaaaaah! Aaaaaah! Yeah, Yeah, take this dick, Kaymee. Oh shit! Fuck!" I growled as I planted my seed deep into her.

My body went limp and my weight fell on her. I rolled over and Kaymee jumped up screaming at me like I did something wrong. I didn't understand why she had an attitude after I just made love to her.

"Fuck you, Dray! You ain't shit! Don't worry about calling me no more because I'm done with your ass!"

I don't know how many times I've told her ass that it wasn't over until I said it was over. Getting up off the bed, I grabbed her by the back of the neck before she could get out the door and slammed her against the wall. I put both hands around her neck and squeezed.

"I can't breathe," I heard her struggle to say. But I didn't let go.

Glancing down in her face, I no longer saw Kaymee. Alexis' eyes were rolling to the back of her head and I let her go quickly. She fell to the floor gasping for air with her hands to her throat. Alexis looked up at me with tears running down her face and snot on her upper lip.

"You are crazy, Dray! If that girl knew what was good for her, she would stay as far away from you as possible. Get some help before you hurt her!" Alexis screamed as she got up and ran out of the room.

Walking out into the living room, I watched her put her coat on and grab her purse. She rushed to the door and I called out to her, "Lexi, I'm sorry. I didn't mean to do that to you."

"Fuck you, Dray. Don't call me anymore," she said as she left my apartment.

Chapter 16
Montez

Kaymee was a damn fool if she thought I believed she didn't know who tried to run her off the road. She has been in this damn city two months and some change, didn't have a damn enemy other than the bitch Dray was fucking with. I didn't think she was crazy enough to do something like what happened to Kaymee.

I took Mee back to her dorm and went to the mall to get ready for my date with Poetry. She didn't want to have anything to do with me but I was ready to show her that I was the only man she needed. How I was going to do that was the problem. It was something I would have to figure out.

Being there for our baby full time was what I needed. I was not going to let her raise my child as a single mother. My mama did that shit when my father left and it was hard as hell for her. Poetry wasn't going to have to endure that pain. She could try to keep fighting it, but she wouldn't win.

Walking through the mall, I was trying to figure out what to buy for my favorite girl. It used to be a time where I could go into a store and buy her anything, but this time was different. I truly didn't know where to start. There was a jewelry store straight ahead and my feet led me in that direction.

I entered the store and as soon as I walked up to the glass case, a beautiful three stone diamond ring caught my eye. The salesperson was helping another customer, but I couldn't stop looking at that ring. Poetry was the only woman I saw myself marrying and having my kids. Getting her to say yes to a proposal at this moment was going to be hard to pull off, but I was willing to give it a shot.

"May I help you, sir?" the woman said, standing behind the counter.

"Yes, can you tell me about this ring right here?" I asked pointing at the ring.

"That's a beauty. It's an emerald-cut diamond encircled with round diamonds, flanked on either side by additional emerald-cut diamonds. Additional round diamonds enlivened the platinum band to complete the look. The ring has a total diamond weight of two carats. The total amount of the ring is—"

"I don't remember asking you how much the ring costs. Do you automatically tell all your customers the price of jewelry?"

"I tell them if they ask—"

"Exactly! I didn't ask, but you felt the need to tell me. Why is it that you had to tell me the price of this ring?"

"Sir, I felt it was my job to tell you the price because it is pricey and I didn't want you to waste your time admiring a ring you can't afford," she had the nerve to say.

"So, you mean to tell me by just looking at me, you just assumed I can't afford this ring? Is it because I am an African American male that stepped into this store wearing baggy jeans, a white t-shirt, sneakers, and a baseball cap?"

Her face got redder than a tomato when I asked her that question. There was three white muthafuckas in the store at the time and they were all wearing a suit of some kind with cufflinks and spit shined shoes, looking like they were born into money but could be the one that would hold this bitch up at gunpoint.

"Excuse me, sir? Did she automatically tell you how much an item was when she assisted you?" The guy looked around and like he was trying to figure out if I was talking to him. "Yeah, I'm talking to you."

"Um, no. She didn't give me a price on anything."

Asking the other two guys the same question, they both had the same response. I turned my attention back to Becky Spot Face and she looked like she was ready to cry. This discrimination shit wasn't about to happen with me. I was willing to cut this shit down at the feet before it escalated into something more.

"So, Sara," I said, reading her nametag. "Where is your manager because you just discriminated against me and you fucked up," I said calmly.

"How is it discriminating when I know for a fact you can't afford this ring?" she said with a smirk on her face.

"You know for a fact, huh? While you're getting your manager, I'll get my money together. As a matter of fact, get ready to wipe the shit off your face." Pulling bands out of my pockets, I counted out ten racks and laid it across the counter. "Not only do I have the money to pay for the ring I was admiring, I also have a black card, bitch," I said, slapping the card on top of the bills. "Now go get your manager!" I yelled.

"I'm sorry—"

"Save that for somebody that gives a fuck. I have nothing else to say to you, *Sara*."

The guys that were in the store were now gone. The jewelry they were looking at, left on the counter, but her attention was on me. They could've walked out that bitch and she wouldn't have known until it was too late. My black ass was the threat, not them.

"What is going on out here?" a young dude asked, coming from the back.

"Sara here felt the need to profile me by the way I dressed and looked. I asked her why she felt the need to tell me the price of this ring," I said, pointing on the glass counter. "Do you know what she said to me?"

"No, I don't, sir," he said as if he didn't give a damn.

"Well, Sara here flat out told me that she didn't want me to waste my time looking at a ring I couldn't afford. She assumed and made an ass out of herself because as you can see, I can damn well pay for that ring. On top of that, she left three white dudes unattended with jewelry that you're lucky enough to still have in your establishment," I said, pointing behind me at the other counters.

He looked around the store, spotting the jewelry that was left out in the open. "Sara, why aren't those pieces locked away?" he asked.

"I left them to assist this gentleman. I knew they wouldn't do anything illegal," she said panicky.

"And how did you know that for sure?"

"They were well-dressed guys—"

"You're just gonna keep sticking your foot in your mouth, Sara. Just admit that you ran over here because you thought I was going to rob the place. It doesn't matter," I said, gathering my money. "I don't want shit out of this muthafucka! You will hearing from my lawyer, as well."

I was throwing it on thick because I was about to get a huge discount on the ring I wanted for Poetry.

"Wait, sir. That won't be necessary. Which ring were you inquiring about?" Before I could say anything, Sara pointed to the piece I asked about. "Such a beautiful piece of jewelry. First, I would like to apologize on my employee's behavior. It shouldn't have happened. Discrimination is against our company policy and it is not tolerated at any time. A lawsuit is the last thing we need. I will do whatever it takes to get that thought thrown away. I am willing to gift this ring to you—"

"Barry, no!" Sara shouted.

"Keep quiet, Sara! You have done and said enough! Like I was saying before I was rudely interrupted, I want to give you this lovely ring for your bride to be," he said, removing it from the case. "what size would you need?" he asked nicely.

"A size six, but you don't have to give it to me," I stated.

"Nonsense, it's my pleasure. This is actually the size you need, so there wouldn't be any need to have it sized. I will box this up for you and you can be on your way. Sara, lock the other pieces up and meet me in my office," he said sternly.

Sara cut her eyes at me and I smiled at her tight-lipped ass. I wasn't looking to get the ring for free, but I wasn't complaining. Free was good where I was from. Watching Sara collect the jewelry and storm to the back, I laughed at her ass. Barry was chewing her ass out and before long, she was running from the back with her purse in hand out the door.

"Here you are, sir, and again, I apologize. I threw in a platinum necklace with a diamond studded angel pendant, as well. Please recommend us to others," he said with a forced smile.

"Thank you," I said, taking the pretty bag and walked out of the store. I wish I would recommend this muthafucka to anybody I said to myself.

Shopping wasn't on my mind anymore because that bull-shit took a lot out of me. I ended up leaving the mall going to the floral shop and buying Poetry two dozen of roses. It was almost six o'clock and I had just enough time to go home and shower.

I arrived at Poetry's door at a quarter to seven and I was cleaner than the board of health. I was sporting a black

Armani shirt, a pair of black slacks, and some comfortable Armani loafers. Holding the roses in one hand with the gift I had for her in my pocket, I was ready.

Knocking on the door, I waited patiently. There was a slight shuffle on the other side before the door opened. Kaymee was standing with a smile on her face when she saw me.

"Aren't you looking good. Come on in. Poe is putting the finishing touches on her makeup. She hasn't had the best day with the morning sickness, but I made her get up anyway," she said, closing the door after I entered.

"Stop telling my business, Mee," Poetry said, walking down the short hall.

She had on a black wrap around maxi dress that hugged her little bump, with a pair of cute gold sandals that showed off her pretty toes. Her hair was styled in a flowy wrap that fell to her shoulders and her makeup was very subtle, just eyeliner and gloss on her lips.

Holding out the flowers, she walked over and accepted them. "These are for you," I said, kissing her cheek. "You look beautiful."

"Thank you. Kaymee, would you put these in water for me? I'll be back a little later. Don't leave to go anywhere without letting me know where you're going. The keys to the truck are on my dresser."

"Yes, mother," Mee said, rolling her eyes. "Don't forget what I said to you either, okay.

"I'll remember as long as you keep your end of the bargain," Poetry said, turning to me. "Are you ready?" she asked.

"Yeah, if y'all are finished talking in codes and shit."

I knew Poetry knew what was going on with Mee. When the time permitted itself, she would open up and tell me about it. Until then, I was going to let both of them think they had one up on me. Poetry walked to the door and I opened it and waited for her to step out before I did the same. We said our goodbyes to Kaymee and we were on our way. We were going to see the *Madea's Farewell* play and I made reservations at a restaurant that would open their doors for us after hours.

"Where are we going that I had to get all dressed up, Montez?" Poetry asked once we were on the road.

I glanced to my right and reached over and grabbed her hand before giving the road my attention again. "We have to be sharp while sitting in the front row of the show. You don't want Madea to clown your ass, do you?"

"Oh my God! You are taking me to see Tyler Perry!" she leaned over and kissed me on the side of my mouth and my pipe bricked up.

It was a small gesture. One that I hadn't experienced in a very long time. A nigga ain't had no pussy in months and I was tired of beating my shit with the palm of my hand. Hopefully, Poe wouldn't take too long to forgive me because I needed sexual healing.

"You love that man and his work. I couldn't pass up the chance to see you laugh just as hard in person as you do while watching him on TV."

"I'm so excited!" she said, squeezing my hand.

I hadn't noticed she was still holding my hand. Lifting it to my lips, I kissed the back of her hand and rested it on my thigh. It felt good to have a sense of closeness with Poetry again. Cherishing this night was what I planned to do. There was no telling how long it would last. Hopefully a lifetime.

***

The show was even funnier in person than it was on TV. Poetry laughed her heart out and it warmed my soul. It felt good to finally put a smile on her face instead of a frown. Every time she slapped my arm and cuddled up against me, my heart sped up. We held hands and talked a little bit during intermission. She even allowed me to rub her stomach a couple times.

It was almost ten o'clock when the show was over. I had already called the restaurant to let them know we were on our way when Poetry went to the bathroom. Getting out of the building was a task and the parking lot was even worse.

"I am so hungry. The nachos I had did nothing for this child of yours."

"I made reservations at Highly Elegance," I said, peeking at her.

"Monty, it's after ten. That place is closed."

"Yeah, I know. But when you got the hook up, it will be open when we get there. It will just be me and you, baby. Sit back and get ready to eat your heart out," I said, smiling.

Parking in front of the restaurant, I got out of the car and went around to open the door for Poetry. As she stepped out, she had a look of surprise on her face. Standing with her mouth open, then closed it abruptly.

"Don't be surprised, Poetry. Let things flow and enjoy the rest of the night. My baby is hungry. Come on," I said, holding her around the waist.

When we entered, there was someone there to seat us immediately. Poetry didn't take her eyes off me after the waiter took our drink orders. She took a deep breath and took a sip of water.

"You did all this for me? But why?" she asked, placing the glass on the table.

"Why not? Poetry, I regret the things that I've done to you and I can't apologize enough. You have shut me out for months and I didn't pressure you into getting back with me. The moment I saw my baby on that screen at the hospital, I knew I had to fight hard for you. Being without you has been the hardest thing I've ever had to do. You were by my side when I had nothing and I want you to be there when I have everything.

Without you, I have nothing. It's time for me to take the wheel and get us back on track. I will do whatever it takes to be back in your good graces. I love you, Poetry Renee and I don't want you to ever forget that. Even if we never get back together, you will forever be my best friend," I said, grabbing both her hands. The tears rolled down her cheeks and I used my thumb to wipe them away.

"When I heard that girl say that y'all had been together two years, that broke me, Monty. I gave you all of me for years only for you to seek something outside of what we had. Knowing that you were unfaithful with one woman for a long period of time made me feel I wasn't good enough for you."

"Poetry, what I did had nothing to do with you. It was me. I don't want you to think any of this was your fault. You were everything to me. I was the nigga that wanted his cake and eat it, too. I knew how old you were when I got with you. When I went places, I knew you couldn't go with me because your parents wouldn't allow it. She didn't have any boundaries, a curfew, parents to answer to. Regardless, I was wrong and I owned up to what I did. I lied and I've been apologizing ever since."

"How am I supposed to trust that you won't do it again if I give you another chance? There may be others out there I know nothing about. One thing I won't be is your fool,

Monty. Through all of this, I've learned that I don't need a man to define me. As much as I love you, I can do it from a distance without laying my heart on the table to get crushed. Our baby doesn't mean we have to be together. We can raise him or her together without being in a relationship."

"In order to trust me, I have to show you that you are all I want. There has never been anyone other than Mena and it was sex between the two of us. I know it hurt to hear that, but I'm being honest with you. She was convenient, available when you weren't. But I had no feelings for her. There's no contact between the two of us and no one else has been in my life. Poetry, let me show you that I love you and only you, baby," I said as my voice cracked.

I knew she was hurt, but I didn't realize she was blaming herself. The emotions I was feeling were foreign to me. There was no coming back from what I did. She was not going to forgive me for breaking her heart.

"You have a lot of proving to do, Monty. I'm not making any promises, but I'm willing to start over. Even though we made a baby together, we have to start from the beginning. You will date me for the second time."

"Whatever you want, I will do," I said as the waiter came over with the food I preordered.

There was steak, lobster, crab legs, chicken fettuccini, macaroni salad, mashed potatoes, corn, broccoli, rolls, and pink lemonade. I made sure she had any and everything she may have wanted. Just like I thought, Poetry went straight for the lobster and crab legs. There were plenty in the back in case she wanted more.

"Are we cool now, Poe?" I asked, cutting my steak.

"Yes, but it won't get back where it was overnight, Montez. There's lots of work to do," she said, snapping the leg of crab.

I took that moment to give her the necklace with the diamond pendant. As I stood and walked around the table, Maxwell's "A Woman's Work" filled the room. I got down on one knee in front of Poetry and pulled the box out of my pocket as she shook her head no repeatedly.

"Monty, no. This is not taking things slow."

"This is a little something I picked up for you. We will take things slow after tonight. Right now, I want to just see your face continue to glow," I said, opening the box.

"Oh my God! Monty, it's beautiful!"

"Not as beautiful as you. You will forever be my angel. You were brought into my life for a reason and I'll be waiting on the day I can spend eternity with you. This is only the beginning of me showing my love."

Taking the necklace out of the box, I stood and Poetry lifted her hair so I could clasp it around her neck. The angel fell above her breast and it looked beautiful against her dark skin. She fiddled with the chain and the smile grew with every second she admired it.

"Don't think material things are going to speed up this union. I'm here to let you know it won't work."

"I have never tried to buy you, Poe. I won't start now."

"Thank you for the gift, Monty. I love it," she said, kissing my cheek.

This kissing on the cheek shit wasn't going to work for me. I didn't have a choice but to take what I could get. I sat back down and started eating again.

"You're welcome. Now, feed my baby," I said, winking at her.

Chapter 17
Dot

Earl had been trying to catch me for weeks. When Kaymee wouldn't give me the money I needed, I tried to go out and get it the best way I could. It didn't work because the crack got the best of me. Now, I was homeless living under the overpass on Wacker Drive. All my shit was sitting on the curb one day I came home. Every muthafucka I'd ever did anything for turned their backs on me. I couldn't find a place to stay for shit. The only thing I had was a damn cellphone and that would be going off soon.

"Get the fuck out of my house, bitch!"

I looked up and Shirley was peeking in her tent. It was cold as hell out here on the street and she wouldn't even share her shit with me. Shirley usually didn't come back for days. I thought I would be good for the night.

"Shirley, don't bring your musty ass over here talking crazy. There's enough room for both of us in here," I said, moving over.

"See, that's where you're wrong. This is my house and I don't want anybody going through my shit. Get out before I drag your ass out. Don't make me fuck you up!"

"All that ain't even necessary. Calm down. I'm getting out," I said, crawling out her dirty ass tent.

"Bring your ass back and I won't give you a warning next time," Shirley said, stepping in my face.

I walked away from her because I was tired and didn't have the strength to whoop her ass. Taking my phone out of my pocket, I dialed my precious daughter's number and waited for her to answer. Kaymee was ignoring me like she had been doing for the past week. Sleeping on the street was getting old and I needed some money. Not only that, the drugs were calling me.

Redialing Kaymee's number, I got the same results and I was getting pissed off. It was about forty degrees and the little ass coat I had on wasn't keeping me warm. I didn't know how I was going to survive another night on the street.

I blocked my number and tried Kaymee again. "Hello," she answered sleepily.

"Kaymee, I need you, baby. I was put out of my apartment and I have nowhere to go. I need you to call a hotel and put it in my name so I can have somewhere to sleep. At least for a month so I can get on my feet," I explained.

"Dot, I'm sorry you are going through that but you have to figure this out on your own. I'm a college student that's going to school on a full scholarship. I don't have any money to get a room for you."

"What the fuck you mean you don't have money to help me? Your daddy has so much fuckin' money, you don't want for shit. Call his ass and tell him you need money, Kaymee!"

"I don't ask my daddy for nothing! I'm a grown ass woman and I take care of myself! Something you should learn to do. You act like I owe you something, Dot. I'm here to let you know I don't owe you shit! If Jonathan's money is what you want, I dare you to call and ask him for it! I'm trying to be as respectful as I can, so don't call me anymore."

"Bitch, I'll come to Atlanta and beat your ass! How dare you talk to me like I'm not your mother!"

"You're not my mother. My mother passed away when I was six. I haven't been loved like that since she left me. Dot, you're nothing to me. Forget that I exist for your sake. When I say I'm tired of the bullshit people think they can keep throwing my way, I'm tired. I could call you a bitch or say fuck you, but I won't.

Karma is working her magic on you for every evil thing you have ever done to me. I won't stoop to your level. You've already hit rock bottom. Seek help and get your life back on track before you kill yourself, Dot. Goodnight because I have class in the morning."

My daughter hung up on me without helping me out. On one hand, I felt her pain but on the other, fuck her. I didn't need her talking to me like she was a damn psychologist or something. I would figure out something, but I wouldn't be calling her ass again.

Pulling my hood over my head to block the wind, I walked in the direction of my old place. It was going to take a minute for me to get there, but I needed a hit. When I got to the building, there was nobody outside. I went inside and one of D's workers was standing in the lobby behind a wall to escape the cold.

"Aye, Dirty. Let me hold a little something 'til next week," I said, walking up on him.

"Dot, yo' ass don't even got a place to lay yo' head. How are you gon' pay me back? Get outta here with all that."

"Come on now. I need some medicine. I'll let you fuck me in the ass," I said to him.

I knew I had his ass thinking about it because his eyes traveled up and down my body slowly. Using what I had to get what I wanted was something I never had to do, but there's a first time for everything. I used to be built like a brick house. Now I was too damn skinny. I would pop this pussy to get a hit, though.

"Man, Dot. I've been wanting to fuck you for years and you never gave me no play. Now you throwing the pussy at a nigga. A'ight, I got you. You better not tell nobody either," he said, walking to the apartment by the elevator.

This was the spot they used when the police were hot on their ass. It was also used for them to fuck these young ass girls that was always hanging around them for money and shoes. And here I was going in for a couple of rocks.

Dirty locked the door behind him and pulled a magnum out of his pocket before dropping his pants to the floor. He had a wad of cash that peeked out his front pocket and my eyes lit up. I knew exactly what I need to do in order to swipe some of it before he noticed.

"Bend over the couch, Dot," he said, stroking his dick.

"I can do on better for you." I stepped out of my pants and bent over grabbing my ankles. My body wasn't the same, but the kitty could make a nigga see in the dark.

"Damn, that thang fat!" Dirty said, running the tip up and down my slit. "Fuck yo' ass. I want this cat!" Guiding his dick into my wetness, my knees buckled. "Where you going? Take this shit."

This young nigga was caressing the hell out of my twat. His pipe was huge and I was loving every second of the hurting he was putting on me. Dirty was fucking me to get a nut. Wasn't nothing lovely about the way he was working me over. Hard pumps were all he was delivering.

I was ready to get high, but the orgasm that threatened to come out of my soul was better than what I was seeking. Squeezing my walls tightly, I felt the pain from his nails digging in my waist. I threw my ass back on him and he growled. I looked over my shoulder and his eyes were shut. It was my chance to rip his ass off and I took it before I missed out.

I got the chance to swipe a bunch of bills and moaned loudly to drown out the crumbling of the bills as I stuffed them on my bra. Dirty pumped into me hard before releasing into the condom. He stepped back and slapped me on the ass before he left out waddling like a duck with his pants at his feet.

"Where are you staying since Earl put you out?" he asked as he flushed the toilet.

"I've been staying wherever I can. Mainly on the street."

"Damn, that's fucked up," he said, walking back into the room. "I'm going to give you some money for a room. Don't go get no damn drugs, Dot! I have you covered on that. It's too cold for you to be sleeping outside. Put my number in your phone."

"My phone will be off in a few days. I don't have money to keep it on."

"Okay, this is what I will do," he said, pulling the money out of his pants. "Fuck that. I can't trust you gon' do right by my money. I'll take you to a motel and pay so you will have somewhere to sleep. Tomorrow I'll pay your phone bill. You lucky your pussy is good because that's the only reason I'm doing this. That pussy will be available anytime I want it. Is that understood?"

"Okay." If all I had to do was fuck this big dick nigga to stay warm, how hard could that be?

He didn't notice that his pockets were a little lighter, so I was cool on that. All I wanted now was to get high. Dirty led me to his car and took me to a decent hotel and paid for a week. When we got to the room, he gave me a hundred dollars worth of crack and a pack of cigarettes. I was in heaven.

"Give me your phone," he said with his hand out. I gave it to him and he put his number in it and called himself. "I'll check on you later. Get some sleep and don't smoke all that shit at once."

Once the door closed behind him, I took the money of my bra and counted it. Six hundred dollars was what I hit him for. I had to make this money last long as possible.

Chapter 18
Kaymee

Acing my finals for the semester was something I was proud of. There weren't any doubts in my mind that I wouldn't do well. I had been spending a lot of time in my dorm unless I was with Poetry or Monty because Dray was still on his power trip. Things had been quiet for the most part, but I didn't want to take any chances.

I was so happy for my two best friends. Monty was going all out to prove that Poetry was the one he loved and wanted forever with. He catered to her every need. Poetry was still having severe headaches and the cause of them were still unknown. At her last appointment, an MRI and CT scan were performed but nothing was abnormal.

"Poe, how are you feeling?" I asked as I sat on the side of her bed.

She had been in bed most of the day because her head was pounding. We kept checking her blood pressure, but that wasn't the issue. The doctor prescribed Tylenol, but the pills only relieved the pain temporarily. Poetry was damn near in tears with her head under the covers.

"I feel like something is stabbing me in my eyes. The back of my head is hurting really bad. Bring me another bottle of water, Mee. I'm going to try another painkiller. Hopefully it will help."

"You took one almost two hours ago, sis. It's too soon to take another one. I'll bring you a hot towel to put across your head. What you need is a good heating pad, though. After I get the towel, I'll fix you a salad and run to Walmart for a pad," I said, standing up.

"Kaymee, call Monty. He will pick one up and bring it over. I don't want you going out alone. Dray has been too quiet," she said, sitting up and massaging her temples. "I think you should tell Jonathan and Monty about the threats."

"He got the picture, sis. Dray has moved on with his life. There's nothing to worry about," I said, leaving out the room.

I made her turkey salad with Italian dressing and took it to her with a bottled water. Telling her I would be right back, I left to go to Walmart. Glancing around the parking lot, I made it to my car with no problem. It felt good to be outside for once. The temperature was pretty mild compared to what it would be like in Chicago. Hopping in the driver's seat, my phone rang and it was Katrina. She had been calling me more than usual asking how I was doing.

"Hey, ma. What's up?"

"Are you driving, Kaymee?"

"I am, but you are connected to the Bluetooth," I said, chuckling.

"Oh okay. I was about to jump in my car to deliver an ass whooping specially for you. I'm calling because we are doing Thanksgiving at the house and I want you guys to make sure you come over."

"Ma, where else will I be for the holiday? I'm not missing out on eating the best meal of the year. Do I need to bring anything?"

"Nope, just yourself, Poetry, and Monty. Your dad is excited to spend this day with you. It's all he's been talking about and it's two weeks away. You should come over and shower him with a little bit of love. How's school coming along?"

"School is good. I aced my finals and now I'm waiting for the next chapter. Jonathan acts like he doesn't call me every other day. I'll spend a couple days with y'all soon. I kind of miss y'all, too," I said, pulling into a vacant spot.

"I'm at Walmart and I don't have my earbuds. I'll call you when I leave. Love you."

"I love you too, lil' girl. Be careful out there," Katrina said before hanging up.

For some reason, an eerie feeling ran through my body. I got out of the car and hit the lock button on my key fob. Entering the store, I grabbed a cart even though I only needed a heating pad. As I moved through the aisles, I felt weird for some odd reason and paranoia was trying to kick in. Dray had me afraid to be in public places nowadays.

When I turned down the linen aisle, I heard footsteps behind me. I swung around and came face to face with a woman that was just surprised as myself. She stepped around me and kept looking back at me, shaking her head.

"Calm down, Kaymee," I muttered to myself.

I started looking at the comforter sets and saw one I liked and put it in the cart. Walking slowly, I noticed the five-dollar DVD bin and raced to hit. I loved the clearance bin in Walmart. I always got the classic movies for little of nothing. Finding six movies I didn't own, I added them to my cart and moved on.

"There she is," I heard a female say behind me.

"Don't start no shit in this store, Alexis."

"I'm not. I need to talk to her. I'm not on that bullshit. Kaymee!" she screamed my name.

Hearing Alexis call my name, I turned around. She was rushing toward me and I didn't have time for the foolishness. I kept walking without acknowledging her. She should know by now that Dray and I are a done deal.

"Can I talk to you for a minute?" she asked, walking beside me. "It's about Dray."

I stopped and looked over at her. "Look, I don't care what you and Dray have going on. He and I are done. So, there's nothing to talk about," I said, pushing my cart forward.

"He's going to hurt you, Kaymee. Please listen to me," she pleaded. This may be too much information for you, but we were having sex and he called out your name. I got mad and told him to get off me. When I got out of the bed, I told him I was done with him and he went berserk.

Kaymee, he grabbed me by the neck and said, 'you ain't gon' leave me, Kaymee. I told you it ain't over until I say it's over.' You have to be careful because he is not the Dray that I know. He is popping pills and drinking lean. There's no telling what that shit has done to his mind."

I listened to her and knew she was telling the truth. The fear in her voice couldn't be faked. "Thank you for telling me. Dray is not going to do anything. He is not crazy," I said, trying to walk away.

"Don't take this lightly. He is capable, Kaymee. I was on the other end of his rant because at that moment, in his mind, I was you! There were a couple times I saw him sitting in his car outside of Abby Hall. Isn't that where you're living? Come on, girl! Open your eyes! Didn't you almost get ran off the road? I know it was him, but here you are playing shit cool. You know like I do that he is crazy! I did my part, now do yours. Watch yourself," Alexis said, walking off.

Pushing the cart to the aisle with the heating pads, I thought about what Alexis said. I was paranoid as hell walking through the store because he could've been there and I didn't know. As I scanned the pads, my phone chimed. It was a message from Dray.

Drayton Montgomery: What did that bitch say to you? You look like you seen a ghost.

Frantically looking around, I didn't see any signs of him. My hands started sweating and I grabbed a pad and threw it in the cart, making my way to checkout. As I put my items on the belt, another notification came through.

Drayton Montgomery: I know where you are. Can you see me? You gon' get enough for ignoring me, Kaymee. You think this a joke? I know Alexis told you what I did to her ass. You next. LOL.

He thought scaring me was funny, but I didn't. His ass was ducked off watching me and I was looking around scared as fuck. The lady in front of me needed to hurry up because I needed to get out of there. My first mind was telling me to leave the shit I had, but Poetry needed that heating pad.

"How are you?" the cashier asked as she began ringing up my items.

"I'm alright and yourself?" I responded, still looking around for Dray.

"I can't complain. Your total is eighty thirty-three," she said cheerfully.

I swiped my card and all but snatched my receipt, racing for the door. Finding my car was something I always had trouble doing when I came to the store. Frantically pushing the button on my key fob, I finally heard the beeping sound I was looking for. I grabbed my bags and threw them in the passenger seat.

"I told you I knew where you were, baby. Why are you trying to leave so fast?"

My body went still as a board when I heard Dray's voice behind me. There was no way I would be able to get in the car without him touching me. I didn't know what to do, so I just stood up straight and faced him.

"Dray, just leave me alone."

"Leave you alone? Leave you alone? Bitch, I'll never just leave you alone! I broke that pussy in and etched my name in it. You my muthafuckin' property now," he snarled.

Knowing he was mad didn't stop me from speaking my mind. I was tired of his threats. Between him and Dot, I wasn't taking their shit anymore. I stood up and stared him in his eye.

"Your property is your car, money, and your kid. I don't belong to nobody! I will not allow you to have me walking around scared for my life. If you're going to do something to me, do it! But when you do whatever you have in mind, you better leave this muthafuckin' country. You won't live to brag about what you've done. And that's not a threat!"

Dray's face hardened and he stepped closer to me. I was bold enough to say those things to him, but I was scared as hell. He grabbed me by the collar of my shirt and banged my back against the doorframe. I winced in pain.

"I don't give a fuck who the fuck come for me, bitch!" he screamed, punching me in the face. "Can't nobody tell me how to handle yo' ass. I told you to stop fucking playing with me!" He punched me again.

The right side of my face went numb and I tasted the blood inside my mouth from my teeth clamping down on my inner cheek. I tried my best to cover my face, but he found an opening, hitting me in the nose. Dray was hitting me like a man and there was nothing I could do about it.

"You gon' do what the fuck I tell you to do or I'm gon' continue to fuck you up!" Punching me in my side, I doubled over, but he pulled me back upright. "I loved yo' ass, Kaymee! But you played me!" he yelled as he slapped me again.

"Stop, Dray! You don't have to do this! Just let me go!" His response was a punch to my left eye. My head hit the top of the doorframe again and I felt my eye swelling.

"Hey! What the fuck is your problem! You don't put your hands on a woman like that!" I heard a woman scream at him.

"Bitch, mind yo' business before I put my hands on you!"

"Oh, don't worry. I'm calling the police on your punk ass! I bet you won't do that shit to a man," she said with her phone to her ear.

"You see what you made me do! I love you and I won't sit back and let you walk away from me. I'm sorry, baby," he said, kissing my cheek and jogged through the parking lot.

I couldn't do anything but cry. Sitting in the driver's seat, I was glad he didn't do more damage than he did. The lady that intervened walked over, still talking on her phone.

"Yes, she is still here. The guy ran off. Okay, thank you," she said into the phone. Are you alright?"

"Thank you. I'm fine."

"His punk ass needs his ass whooped. The police are on the way, but that don't matter. You better call your brothers, daddy, cousins, uncles, shit, your ex boyfriends because he won't buff up at them. I can't stand a nigga that puts his hands on a female! That shit burns me up! You don't allow a nigga to use you as a punching bag." The woman was going off for what happened to me. "Your eye is going to be black."

My phone started ringing and Poetry's name appeared on the screen. I was crying, so I knew she was going to be able to tell. I had to answer so she wouldn't be worried, even though I didn't want to. She may as well find out now rather than when I walked through the door at the dorm.

"Hello," I sniffed.

"Kaymee, what's wrong? You've been gone for a while," she said worriedly.

"Dray—"

"That's all I needed to hear. Are you still at Walmart?" she asked, cutting me off.

"Yes, don't call anybody, Poe. The police are on their way," I said, knowing she wasn't going to listen to me.

"Kaymee, you sound dumb as hell! Don't tell the police shit! His punk ass already know how things are handled around these parts. I'll call you back."

Poetry didn't give me a chance to argue with her about calling Monty. I knew exactly what she did when she hung up on me. Dray brought this on himself and I was at fault for not telling anybody the severity of what was going on. He could've beat me to death if the woman hadn't come to my aid.

"I'll stay here with you until the police show up. I'm a nurse and I have ice packs in my car. It's right over there," she said, pointing to her car.

Watching her walk away, my phone rang. I glanced down, closing the door. This was going to be bad on Dray's part. He fucked up this time. When I answered, Monty's voice boomed through the speaker.

"That nigga dead, Mee! I wanna know every mutha-fuckin' thing he has been saying and doing to you today! You will not keep lying for this nigga! He don't give a fuck about you! Poetry told me the police was on their way. We don't do them niggas! Dray's ass will be handled and I'm on my way!"

Monty hung up and I saw two squad cars drive into the parking lot fast. The woman that helped me flagged them down and pointed in my direction. I could barely see out of my left eye and it was hurting with every tear that dropped. One of the officers walked over to my car and I opened the door and got out.

"Ma'am, tell me what happened," he said.

"I came out of the store and a man came up to me being irate. I think he was on drugs or something because he was calling me someone else's name. He grabbed me by my shirt and punched me a few times. I cried out for him to stop, but he wouldn't. It was like he couldn't hear me. The woman over there scared him away when he said she was calling the police." I told him the truth but lied at the same time. The woman brought the ice pack to me and I placed it on my eye.

"You didn't know this guy?" the officer asked.

"No, I've never seen him before. I'm from Chicago and I came here to attend Spelman College. I haven't had a chance to meet anyone here. I'm trying to figure out why did he choose me," I said, crying. The tears were real because I was in pain. I was glad because it made the story believable.

"Do you need to go to the hospital? Your eye looks pretty bad."

"No, I'll be okay. I just want to go back to my dorm," I said, shedding more tears.

"Is there someone that can come drive you because your eye is almost closed shut?"

"Yes, my brother is on his way," I explained.

"Well, that's all I need to know. I'm going to need your identification so I can document this, I'll have a report for you in a few minutes." I retrieved my purse and gave him my license. "Thank you, sit tight," the officer said, walking to his car.

I saw Monty's car driving slowly over a speed bump before he parked his car in the aisle behind me. He was probably waiting for the police to leave because he didn't get out. He had his phone to his ear, but his mouth wasn't moving. There was someone else in the car with him, but I didn't know who it could be.

After about ten minutes, the officer came back and handed me a police report. "If there are any more incidents, I want you to give us a call. This really sounds like a random act but be careful, young lady. Take care and try to enjoy the rest of your day," he said, walking away.

As soon as the police car left the parking lot, Monty and the person in the car with him got out making their way to me. I turned and held my head down so he couldn't see my face, but it didn't help. He opened the door and stooped down next to me.

"Look at me, Mee," he said calmly. I shook my head no and a tear fell down my face. "Let me see your face, man." When I turned to look at him, his eyes widen with surprise.

"It's not as bad as it looks."

"He put his muthafuckin' hands on you, sis! I'm not letting this shit ride!" he said, standing up. "Los, drive her shit and follow me." I got out of my car and walked toward Monty's car. "Where you going? Get in the passenger side of *yo'* shit! With you still justifying what this nigga been doing to you, I don't want to be nowhere near you right now," he said, brushing past me.

"Monty!" I yelled at his back, but he kept going.

"Come on, ma. Get in the car."

I'd realized the person with Monty was Los. There was no reason to hide my face from him because he had already saw it. He walked me around to the passenger side and opened the door. Once I got comfortable in the seat, he closed the door and walked around the car to get in. I was waiting for him to start the car up because he was just sitting there.

"Give me your keys, ma," he said, holding out his hand. I grabbed my purse from the floor and gave them to him.

He started the car and pulled off. Honking at Monty, Los waited until he pulled out to follow him. Instead of taking a right out of the parking lot, Monty went left. It didn't take a rocket scientist to know that he was leading Los to my daddy's house. I hurried up and dialed his number before we got too far away from my dorm.

Keeping an eye on Monty as the phone rang, I literally saw him glance down and put the phone away. I tried calling again and he didn't bother to look. The last thing I wanted was for Jonathan to see my face. The ice pack was still cold, so I put it back on my eye.

"Would you turn around and take me home, please?" I asked Los nicely.

"I can't do that. This has to happen, Kaymee. Jonathan has a right to know what happened to you. Hiding things from yo' people is fucked up. Dray needs his ass beat, ma. You are better than that. His ass sees how strong you are and he is only trying to break you down. You don't need an insecure ass nigga that's for everybody and don't know how to keep his hands to himself."

Los was right, but I didn't want to hear all of that. I just wanted to go home. "Look, I just want to go home. Poetry needs this heating pad and I've been gone long enough,"

"Don't worry about Poetry. She's good. Monty talked to her already. How do you think we found out what happened? How's your eye?"

"The shit hurts! That's how it is!" I yelled.

"Don't get mad at me. I was only showing concern for yo' ass. You don't have to worry about me saying shit else," he said, turning the radio on.

"I'm sorry. I shouldn't be mad at you."

Los didn't respond as he bobbed his head to the song that was playing. I laid my head on the window and closed my eyes, preparing myself for the moment my daddy saw my face. We pulled up to the house as soon as I opened my eyes. I had drifted off to sleep.

Monty was standing outside the door waiting for someone to open it. My daddy opened the door in a wife beater, basketball shorts, and a pair of slides on his feet. I couldn't hear what was being said, but Monty gestured toward the car and my daddy stormed over. Los popped the locks before he got to the car and he snatched the door open.

"I know you muthafuckin' lying! I told that nigga if he didn't want to do right by you to bring yo' ass back to me or call me to come get you! His ass is dead!" my daddy yelled, while looking at my face. "Come in the house, baby girl. I want you to tell me everything and don't leave shit out. I'm going to tell you this one time, I despise a liar, so don't test me!"

Being pissed was an understatement. He was foaming at the mouth, so I new he was hot. I got out of the car and walked slowly up the stairs. When I got inside, my daddy was pacing back and forth in the living room. Los came in and closed the door behind him and stood against the wall.

"Where is this nigga, Kaymee?" my daddy asked loudly.

"Calm down, bae," Katrina said from the couch.

"Calm down! Do you see her fuckin' face? Let me handle this my way!"

I directed his attention back to me because I didn't want him to be mad at Katrina. "I don't know where he is. I told him I was done with him a while ago. He showed up at Walmart talking crazy and when I stood up to him, he hit me," I tried to explain.

"Kaymee, shit like this didn't just start happening. Stop playing me for a fool because you are not telling me the full story. I want to know what happened prior to today!"

"I found out he was dealing with another girl when I first got here. The verbal abuse and threats started that day," I said, watching Monty shake his head. "I avoided him every chance I could by blocking him from my phone. He started sending messages through my social media messenger. I didn't take what he said seriously because all he was doing was talking—"

"When he came to the hospital the day Poetry fainted, he took you outside and threatened you?" Monty asked.

"Yes," I said lowly.

"That nigga was scaring the shit outta you and I was right inside! His punk ass would be a distant memory by now if yo' ass hadn't been mum mouthed about the shit!" Jonathan screamed. "Let me ask you this since we are playing the truth game. Was he the person that tried to run you off the road?" he asked, folding his arms over his chest. Monty leaned in, waiting on my response with his hand on his hip.

"Yeah, it was him," I said, wringing my hands.

"Keeping shit from me could've gotten you killed! Ain't nobody worth losing your life over, Kaymee! His dick ain't that important for you to be trying to save his ass! I'm not gon' tolerate a muthafucka doing mine wrong and I won't let you be out here looking stupid for his bitch ass either! Open the messages so I can see what the fuck he had to say to you," he said, holding out his hand.

I couldn't do nothing except let them read the shit. Both he and Monty were mad as fuck and I didn't want to keep anything else from them. Whatever they had for Dray was on him. Giving him the phone, I walked to the bathroom down the hall. Before I could close the door, Katrina came in and hugged me.

"Your father loves you and when you hurt, he hurts. It's his job to protect you, but you have to tell him when there's something going on that's out of control. Kaymee, have you seen your face? Look at yourself," she said, turning me toward the mirror. "That's not love, baby," she said with tears in her eyes.

"Katrina, I told him I didn't want anything to do with him before any of this happened. He is mad because I'm not fucking with him! I didn't ask for him to do this to me! Dray won't leave me alone, not the other way around! I didn't say anything because I just got my daddy back in my life and I don't want him going back to jail behind my shit!" I said, crying hard.

"I know how you feel, baby. Don't beat yourself up. Everything will work out," she said, leaving out the bathroom.

Staring at myself in the mirror, I looked like I had a fight with Lenard Lewis or somebody. My eye was yellow, red, and black. That negro had me looking like a German flag. I took my foundation out of my purse and started covering up the bruises. It didn't help much because my eye was sitting out like a golf ball. Leaving out the bathroom, I heard Monty's voice.

"I'm killing his ass, Jonathan. I warned him ahead of time. His punk ass ain't answering his phone because he knows I'm one,"

"He has to drop my money off at some point," my daddy said.

"I wouldn't be surprise if he run off. I'm not trying to throw dirt on your shit, but he knows he fucked up. That's why he's dodging calls," Monty said, looking up as I entered the room.

"I read all of those messages and I think you and Poetry should stay here for a little while," Jonathan said. "He will try to take another strike at you if given the chance."

"The girl Alexis told me he was using Molly and drinking lean. I think he is using more drugs than he's selling. Your money is going to be short regardless. She should know where to find him. She lives on campus, so it shouldn't be hard to find her. I'll be upstairs," I said, leaving them to plan whatever they had in mind.

Chapter 19
Drayton

Nosy bitch! I should've whooped her ass too for getting in my business. I had to get away from there before twelve showed up because I wasn't trying to get locked up. When I got to my car, I sped out of the lot and hit the corner without checking for traffic and almost side swiped a damn truck. My anxiety was through the roof. Lifting the armrest, I fished around blindly until my hand found the bag of Mollies. I popped one in my mouth and I knew I was going to be good when it kicked in.

My dependency of pills was getting out of control. It first started when I got the news that Melody was pregnant. I wasn't ready to be a father to nobody! Playing the happy first daddy role with Melody was hard. I thought about kicking her ass down a flight of stairs daily. When I tried to stay away from her, she called, I went.

One would think if the drugs were making me do things and have thoughts of doing stupid shit, I would cut out the problem. I wanted to, but I was in too deep. There wasn't a day that went by that I couldn't have the Molly or lean.

Harassing Kaymee was never in the plans. It just happened. All I wanted was the love we shared back in Chicago and she took that from me. Knowing Los had his eye on her made matters worse. She was not going to be with anyone else and walk around happy while I was miserable. For some reason, the fear in her eyes when she saw me and the shiver in her voice when she talked, made me brick up.

It took about fifteen minutes for me to get to my apartment. The pill had relaxed me and I went straight to the bar and mixed a cup of lean. My phone started vibrating in my pocket and it was Monty. Word had gotten out about what

I'd done to 'Little Miss Innocent'. I let the voicemail pick up without answering. He called four more times and gave up.

Kaymee was so pure that she didn't see any of the things I said as a problem. She was nothing like Alexis and Melody. Those two spoke their minds without thinking. Kaymee, on the other hand, bowed down to everything I said. Now I was stuck between a rock and a hard place because her daddy and Monty were going to be out for blood.

It was a good thing I had never invited her to my place. They wouldn't know where to start looking for me. I didn't have to worry about them finding me on the campus of Morehouse because I stopped attending school months ago.

Before all of this shit with Kaymee got out of hand, I already knew Jonathan was going to be a problem. I was eating his pills like candy and I didn't have a dollar to give him. The only money I had was what I had saved. I could live for a long time off the money because I was getting high for free. I didn't have to pay for the shit I was using regularly. They would come for me to pay with my life, but they would have to find me first.

I sat sipping the lean, trying to come up with a plan. Getting out of Georgia was my first thought. Where I would go was the issue. My thoughts were to go back to my parents that I hadn't seen in about a year. Thanksgiving was a couple weeks away and I was going to use that as an excuse to go visit them. I grabbed my phone and dialed my parents' number.

"Hello," my mother sang into the phone.

"Hey, Beautiful! How's my favorite girl?"

"I'm doing wonderful. I haven't heard from you in forever, Drayton. I'm glad you called. Your father was just talking about you. Saying you are too busy getting turned into a man at Morehouse. I am so proud of you, baby," she said as happy as she could be.

"Dad knows there's no time for anything but hard work. I will do better with calling you and dad. Enough about me, what are you cooking for Thanksgiving?"

"Well, it's a couple weeks away but I have my list right here," she said, shuffling through papers. "I'm making mac and cheese, Cajun fried turkey, ham, Cornish hens, potato salad, coleslaw, sweet potatoes, collard and mustard greens, chitterlings, dressing, green beans, dinner rolls, and a slew of cakes and pies."

"Man, ma! You about to cook it up! Are you hosting at the house this year?" I asked.

"Yes, I am. Last year was a disaster! Your aunt Darlene made those gritty ass greens and I almost died! I didn't eat anything from that damn house. Got all them damn cats and invited folks over with cat hair over everything. It was a mess. I wish you were coming home. I would love to see you."

"Well, your wish just came true because I was calling to tell you that I will be coming home tomorrow," I said, taking a sip from my cup.

"Drayton Senior! My baby is coming home!" she yelled to my father.

I didn't want to talk to my dad because he always knew when something was going on with me. I wasn't in the mood to be interrogated by him. "Mom, I have some calls to make, but I will see you tomorrow. Love you," I said, trying to get off the phone before my father made it to whatever room she was in.

"I love you too, baby. Your father is on his way downstairs. You know he's going to want to talk to you."

"I know, ma, but I'll call back a little later. Let me take care of this business first."

"Okay, baby. Take care."

I hung up before she could start talking about anything else. I stared at my phone and dreaded the call I had to make to Melody. We weren't in a relationship or even having sex, but she was adamant about me being in our child's life. This was my out and I was about to take it without her knowledge. I pressed the phone icon under her name and waited for her to answer.

"Hey, Dray," she said with an attitude.

"What's wrong with you?"

"You missed my appointment! I told you what time it was and you didn't even have the decency to show up!"

"Damn, I forgot about that. I had something to take care of. It slipped my mind."

"Dray, I'm tired of repeating the same shit to you over and over. I need you to be here for this baby. If you can't make appointments that has to do with our bay's health, how am I supposed to know that you are going to be here when he is born?"

"Oh, you found out you're having a boy!" I said with no excitement in my voice.

"No, *we* are having a boy!" she screamed.

"Look, I didn't call to argue with you, Mel. I wanted you to know I have to go out of town on business for a couple months. Facetime me for your next appointment and it will be like I'm right there with you."

"You want me to Facetime you to spend time with your son when he's born, too? Is that how you plan on being in his life?"

"Mel, you are taking this way to far now. I will be back before you know it. There's money to be made and I'm about to get it," I lied.

"Whatever, Dray. I don't know what's going on with you, but get it together," she said, hanging up.

I wanted to call her back, but fuck Melody. She could take care of the baby by herself. Her place wasn't safe for me because Monty knew where she lived. I wasn't worried about him coming to my parents place because all he knew was, I was from Massachusetts.

I went online and looked up flights. There was a flight leaving that night at nine. Booking a one-way ticket home, I also made reservations at the Hyatt for a few weeks. I was not about to deal with my parents trying to tell me what I could and couldn't do in their home.

Finishing my drink, I went into my room and packed my luggage. I had two large bags that held clothes and shoes. I walked into the closet and opened the safe I had on the floor. It was filled with money that I had rubber banded in bundles. Placing all the money in the bag, I closed it and put it with the others.

I would have to come back to get my car and drive back once things died down. For now, I had to secure my apartment for the time being. My checkbook was in my luggage and I walked over and pulled it out. I wrote a check for eighteen hundred dollars to pay my rent up for two months. That would give me enough time to disappear for good.

Chapter 20
Poetry

Thanksgiving at Jonathan's house so far was one to remember. The entire Goon squad was present with their wives and kids. I was happy to see Kaymee having a good time with people that loved her. Even though the reason behind them showing up was to find Dray and kill him. Monty had been looking for him high and low, but it was like he vanished into thin air.

I met Nova, Jade, Monica, and Scony's twin sisters, MaKayla and MaKenzie. They are all strong-minded women that gave Kaymee sound advice on her situation. I could tell all of them had a story to tell and I couldn't wait to hear about it. The men in their lives are such distinguished gentlemen with a pound of thug in them.

Scony's son, Malikhi, wouldn't leave my side the entire time we were around him. Katrina said that was a sign that I was having a girl. She explained the saying of, if a boy clings to you while pregnant, you're having a girl. If a girl wants nothing to do with you, you're having a girl. I think she was right because G's daughter, Ryleigh, hollered when I tried to hold her, but I kept trying and failed.

We all got full and watched football with the guys before us girls went out to a movie. I got to know them and we agreed to stay in touch. When the night was over, I ended up staying the night with Montez. My hormones had been raging out of control and my vibrator wasn't doing it anymore.

After taking a shower, I laid in his bed until he finished showering. When he walked out of the bathroom with only a towel wrapped around his waist, my lady parts started doing the salsa. From the food he brought without being asked and the flowers that were delivered to my dorm every day, to the amazing foot and back massages he gave me whenever needed. Montez was getting this kitty.

My eyes followed his every move and my nipples hardened. At that moment, my baby wanted to cockblock from the womb and kicked the hell out of me. I looked down because I had never felt it that strong before. There would be little pats here and there, but never like that. Shifting a little bit on the bed, the little devil kicked again.

"Owww!" I screamed, sitting up.

Montez rushed over and sat down. "What's wrong?"

"Your baby kicked me hard as hell, twice!"

"It's nothing new. I feel it kick all the time. There's nothing to worry about. Lay back and let me rub my baby. That's what you get for eating everything you saw earlier," he said, laughing. The minute he put his hand on my stomach, there was another kick. "Oh shit! You could see your stomach expand with that one!"

He was excited to see the baby moving around. It felt like he or she was doing a stretch exercise. While he thought it was cute, the shit was hurting me. Montez kept rubbing the spot that protruded out and the baby would move to another location. I let it go on for about five minutes until I couldn't take it anymore.

"That's enough! It hurts! I shouldn't have been thinking about jumping your bones," I said, the last statement slipping out.

"Oh, so you want to use my body, huh?" he said, grinning

"You didn't hear that," I said, lying down.

"I know what I heard, Poe," he said, bringing his mouth to my left nipple.

Montez licked around my areola and I almost came instantly. It had been so long since he touched me sexually and I was ready for it. Massaging between my legs, he found my bud and I opened wide for him. He kissed his way down and replaced his finger with his tongue. My back arched a little bit and my hands held his head in place.

"Ooooooo," I moaned, closing my eyes.

Slurping on my wetness, he was moaning into my kitty, not missing a drop. He started caressing the top of my mound as he stuck his tongue into my tunnel. It was a major hot spot of mine and he knew it. His lips felt good sucking my lips and going back to my clit. Gripping both my legs in the crook of his arms, he sucked hard on my clit.

"Aaaaah, shit!" I moaned loudly as I tried to get away.

He shook his head no, while looking at me with those pretty brown eyes. Sticking his fingers in my honey pot, I moved my hips back and forth to help him out. I felt my orgasm building and it was going to be a big one. I rode his fingers like it was a dick and he continued to feast on my goods.

"Yes, Monty! Don't stop! Right there! Suck harder!"

I was giving him instructions because I needed him to be precise with his shit. He started sucking the way he knew I liked and I lost all control. I grabbed the back of his head and let my juices flow like a Gerald Levert song down his throat. He eased up my body licking his lips while smirking at me. Kissing my lips, I opened my mouth and invited his tongue to enter.

My nectar tasted good and I could smell the scent on his face. He broke our kiss and laid on his side, propping his hand on the side of his head. My body was so relaxed after the tongue-lashing he had given me.

"What got you over there smiling and shit? Montez asked.

I didn't realize I was smiling to be honest. I was watching as the plane glided through the clear skies, then my mind flashed back to Thanksgiving night. Everything that was happening around me didn't exist to me.

"I wasn't thinking about anything." I blushed refusing to look at him.

"I already know what your mind was on. I just need to know which session got your face heating up," he whispered in my ear.

Monty and I were going to Chicago to spend Christmas with my parents. Then we were going to Vegas to get away for a couple days. Kaymee claimed she didn't want to be the third wheel and refused to come with us. I, myself, believed she was trying to spend time with Los. I noticed they'd become real friendly with each other since Thanksgiving.

At six months pregnant, I looked like I swallowed a small watermelon. The seats weren't very comfortable but I was happy to be away with Montez. I didn't know why he chose to take me to Vegas because I wasn't old enough to gamble. Whenever I asked, he told me to just get ready to enjoy myself and stop asking so many questions.

"We will be landing soon. Please put on your seat belts and bring your seats to the upright position. We will be landing at Midway airport in approximately fifteen minutes. Welcome to the Windy City. The temperature is a freezing twenty-five degrees and windy. Thank you for flying Southwest Airlines," the stewardess announced.

I was glad that we were in the front of the plane because I didn't feel like being cooped inside, waiting for everyone to get off. When we landed, Montez grabbed our bags from the overhead and waited for me to exit the plane. It felt good to be back in my hometown, but I wanted to turn around and go right back down south. I was so glad that I bought a heavy coat and gloves online because the hawk was out.

Montez rented a car and when I stepped out of the doors of the airport, my teeth started chattering together. We both jumped in the car like the air was speaking a foreign language. It was so disrespectful for it to be so cold.

"I don't remember being this cold when I lived here. This is a different kind of cold and I don't like it," I whined as I reached out and turned the heat up to the max.

"I'm gon' have to agree with you this time, bae. We will be here for two days, then off to Vegas we go. It is so much warmer there."

Monty pulled out into traffic after the car warmed up and headed toward my parents' home. His cellphone rang and he glanced down and picked it up. He wasn't saying much, but it didn't bother me like it would have earlier in the year. I've learned in the short time we've been back together, to trust him. He hasn't given me any reason not to.

Ending the call, he glanced at me, "That was —"

"Monty, you don't have to keep telling me who's calling you. I trust you not to ever disrespect this relationship again. You have been given a second chance. There won't be a third."

"Yeah, I already know you have me on permanent lockdown. Now hush all that shit up. That was Kaymee. She said take your phone off airplane mode," he said, smiling.

I took my phone from my purse and as soon as I took it off airplane mode, it rang. "Hey, sis!" I said cheerfully.

"Girl! Tell me why Los wants me to go with him to something called Illuminate at Sugarloaf Mall. I don't know if I want to go out on a date with anyone so soon after Dray."

"Kaymee, fuck Dray! Life is too short for you to be limiting yourself to a nothing ass nigga that shitted on you! Why do it have to be a date? There is a thing called two people going out to enjoy the holidays together. I think you should go. You have been spending your time in the house or with Jonathan and Katrina. Keep on the way you are and you will be old before your time."

"I'll think about it, but I want you to stop going in on me, mother hen," she said, laughing.

"There's nobody that's going to speak truth to you better than me. All I'm saying is don't waste your life being scared to take a chance. There is so much to see out here in this dreadful world. Live your best life, sis."

"Yeah, you're right. How have you been feeling?" she asked seriously.

"Other than feeling bloated, I'm good," I lied.

"Well, I'll call you later. I'm about to text Carlos and tell him I will take him up on his offer," she said giddily.

"Oh, he's Carlos now," I said, chuckling as I turned my head away from Montez. "Have fun and I want to hear all about it."

"Whatever, you have fun, too. I can't wait to hear about your trip! Okay, talk to you later," she said, hanging up.

I was trying my best to appear normal. My head was killing me, but I didn't want to worry Monty. The past couple times I went to the doctor, Monty and I explained my severe headaches. Dr. Brim ran every test known to man from CT scans to MRIs and couldn't determine what was causing them. To be truthful, I was really scared of not knowing what was going on with me.

We turned onto my parents' street and I was happy because I just wanted to relax. Monty parked in the driveway, shutting the car off. He got out of the car, grabbed our bags from the back, and came to open the door for me to get out. I fished around in my purse and pulled out my keys. I didn't tell my parents what time I was coming, so I hope I didn't scare the hell out of my mama when I walked in her house unannounced.

Before I could stick the key in the door, it opened. "I know you weren't about to enter my home without ringing the bell," my mama said with a smile on her face.

"Yes, I was! It's too cold to be standing here waiting on somebody to open the door." I smiled back. "Let me in, woman! It's cold!" I said, hugging her and pushing my way inside at the same time.

The house was nice and warm, just like I remembered during this time of the year. Mama let me go and turned to Montez and opened her arms wide for a hug. Once all the hugs were out of the way, her eyes landed on my baby bump. She had seen it when I called her on Facetime, but I guess it was different seeing it up close and personal.

"I can't believe my baby is having a baby!" she said, placing her hands on my stomach. "I started buying things for my grandbaby. I'm so excited, but I will show you the gifts later. Come on so we can relax in the living room. Your father is in his office wrapping up a conference call. Monty, leave those bags there, baby," she said over her shoulder.

Sitting in my father's favorite recliner, I let it back and relaxed. I looked around the room and the Christmas spirit were all around. The six-foot tree sat in the corner by the window. My mother used silver and blue décor. I couldn't wait until later because I would be sitting right in the recliner when the timer turned the lights on.

My father's chair was comfortable and I didn't realize I had dozed off. Opening my eyes, my vision was blurry and the back of my eyes felt like something was stabbing me. I tried to sit up and fell back, closing my eyes again. I didn't know where everyone went, but I had to get to the kitchen for some water. I had medication in my purse my doctor prescribed and they worked wonders.

After a few minutes, I was able to get up. Fighting through the pain, I made it to the refrigerator and back to the recliner. Taking one of the pills, I ended up going back to sleep. Something had to give because I didn't know how much longer I could deal with the pain.

Chapter 21
Monty

Poetry's mom Chris was cool. We sat and talked about the baby and how things were going between Poetry and I. I knew how close she was to her daughter and there was no use in lying. If I had any chance of keeping a good relationship with her parents, honesty was the way to go.

"I'm glad you guys worked things out. When Poetry called and said she was pregnant, I was mad at first because I didn't want that for her, but an abortion was out of the question," she said, glancing over at Poetry who had fallen asleep. "This was something that you two made together, now you have to handle it together. I too was a teenaged mother, but it's harder now."

"Mrs. Chris, I love Poetry. She won't have to raise this baby on her own. I know how it feels to be without a father and I don't want that for my child. You have my word that I will do what's right for both of them. I'm lucky she let me back in her life as more than the father of our baby. I messed up, I'll admit that. It won't happen again. She means the world to me and I jeopardized not only our relationship, but our friendship, as well."

"You better not have my baby crying no damn mo', I know that much," her father said, walking into the room. He walked to the chair Poetry was lying back in and kissed her on the head. Walking to the loveseat across from where I was sitting, he sat down and crossed his foot over his knee. "Finding out my baby was with child pissed me off. I was on my way to Atlanta to kick your ass. You are lucky my wife talked me down because you were a goner. What are your plans?" he asked.

"I plan to be there for her and the baby. By being there, I will support her anyway possible. I will fix my schedule to accommodate her and the baby. One thing I don't want is my baby going to anyone's daycare. I will be a hands-on dad for sure. Nothing will come before them," I answered his question, looking him in the eyes.

"That's good to know, but those weren't the plans I were referencing to. I'm not the type of man to water down anything in life, so you know I'm not going to do it about my daughter. You laid down and had sex with her, ya'll made a baby and live separately. When are you going to make an honest woman out of her?"

I glanced at Poetry and knew she was sleeping but didn't know how hard. "About that, I wanted to talk to you in private if that's okay," I said nervously.

"Yeah, come on. I want to hear what you have to say," he said, getting up and walked out the room.

"I'm going to start dinner while the two of you talk. By the way, Monty. How have Poetry's headaches been lately?" Mrs. Chris asked.

"They are off and on. We had tests done, but the doctors still can't figure out what's causing them. We're not giving up, though."

"I'm going to continue doing research because I don't like not knowing what's going on. Keep me posted because when I ask Poetry anything, she tries to shy away from the subject."

"I'll make sure to do that," I responded.

"Okay, well get on up there before the grouch comes looking for you. He's in Poetry's old room. You know where it is," she grinned.

"Yes, ma'am."

Climbing the stairs slowly, I'd admit that I was nervous as hell. This was the reason I arranged for us to come to Chicago first then Vegas the day after Christmas, so I could have a heart to heart with her father. I wanted him to know that Poetry was safe with me and I would be there through everything. Taking a deep breath at the top of the stairs, I moved to the opened door of his office.

"Come in and have a seat," he said from behind his desk.

The room looked a lot different from the last time I was in it. The images of what transpired between these walls had me beaming on the inside. I had to shake my head to push my thoughts back. That wasn't the time to be reminiscing on the past.

"Mr. Parker, I want you to know—" I began but he cut me off.

"Look, Monty. I've known you for years. From the first time my daughter started coming home from school like she won the lottery every day, I knew you meant a lot to her. As much as I tried to stop her from being around you, she wouldn't listen. I never had any problems with you putting your hands on her that I know of. Nor have she said anything negative about you. When you stepped out on y'all relationship, she was truly hurt but she did not tarnish your name. She weathered that storm like a very mature young lady.

My daughter is wise beyond her years and I'm not saying that because I'm her father. I spoke those words from the moment I brought her home from the hospital. You have some pretty big shoes to fill because I was her first love. I taught her how she should be treated and I'm glad she listened. Now again, what are your plans?"

He had said a mouthful and my level of respect grew greatly for him. "When Poetry and I leave the day after Christmas, we are heading to Vegas. I wanted to talk to you because she thinks we're going just to have the experience. My reason for going is to marry her. I know you probably already have her wedding planned, but I want to do it this way.

I almost lost her once. I don't plan to ever let her go again. My child will have my last name and I want her to have it, too. I will always love, honor, and cherish Poetry for the rest of my life. I'm going back to tradition. Do I have your permission to marry your daughter?"

Stan was quiet for what seemed like a long time with his head down. When he looked up at me, he had tears in his eyes. I sat without speaking because I wanted him to respond when he was ready.

"I heard myself in the words that you spoke. My speech was almost identical to yours when I approached Christine's father about the same subject. We have been together almost two decades and Poetry is what got us where we are today. I too messed around and had to beg and plead only to get turned down. I spent so much money trying to win her love back," he said, laughing as he wiped his face with a tissue. "You are good for her Monty. I have faith that you will do right by my baby. You have my permission, but please don't make me out of a liar," he said, coming around the desk and embracing me in a brotherly hug. "Congratulations, son."

"Thank you. I will make you proud."

"There's one more thing I need to know. Where is the ring? My daughter is a princess and I have to make sure you got her right."

I went in my pocket and pulled the ring box out. Before I opened it, I looked up at Stan and smirked. "Poetry has never been a princess in my eyes. She will forever be the queen of my heart," I said, lifting the lid of the box.

He whistled loudly, taking the box from my hand. "You did damn good with this one. Yeah, she got yo' ass wide open, but she deserves this motherfucker," he said, handing it back. "Congratulations again, Monty. All you have to do is be honest, give her attention, and don't lie. I'll give you some tips on a successful marriage before you leave. Join me on the back for a celebratory cigar."

"Ummm, Stan. I don't think the cigars I smoke are allowed."

"You smoke what you smoke, and I'll smoke what I smoke. No judgment here," he said, walking out the room.

"'Nough said. I gotta run out to the car," I said, hitting him on the back.

***

Poetry slept for a long time when we arrived at her parent's house. After hanging out with her father, I went into the kitchen to give her mama a hand with dinner. She didn't cook a ton of food for the holiday. She made a pot of mostaccoli, garlic bread, and sweet peas.

"My daughter got her a man that knows his way around the kitchen," her mama laughed.

"I know how to do a little something. We won't starve, I can promise you that," I said, putting the bread in the oven. "I'll wake Poe so she can eat. She should be good and hungry," I said as I left the kitchen.

"Tell her dinner will be ready in ten minutes," I heard her yell out.

My baby looked so comfortable in that damn chair. Poetry had been sleeping for over three hours. I leaned down and kissed her all over her face. She stirred a bit then slowly opened her eyes.

"Hey, sleepyhead. How you feeling?"

"I feel a lot better than earlier. My head is no longer hurting, so that's a good thing. Mmmm, something smells good!" she said, sniffing the air. "My mama cooked Mostaccoli, didn't she?" she asked excitedly.

"Yes, she did and it's good, too."

Poetry looked at the Christmas tree and lit up like a little kid. I knew Christmas was her favorite holiday of all time. Helping her stand to her feet, she walked over and watched the lights flashing at different speeds and with several beautiful pattern sequences.

"Baby, get my parents' gifts out the car and put them under the tree as I wash up? We will be opening gifts and singing carols after dinner," she said with a big smile.

I loved how they had a tradition that never changed throughout the years. Growing up, I didn't have that. My mama did the best she could with the little she had. Making a better life for us was the reason I turned to the streets. I was tired of seeing her struggle financially.

"Sounds good. Go wash up. The tree will still be here when you get back," I told her as I headed for the door.

When I came back in with the bag that held the gifts, everyone was sitting at the table waiting for me to return. Poetry smiled at me as I placed the wrapped gifts under the tree. I went to the bathroom to wash my hands because I was ready to get eat. Stan said grace when I sat down and everyone started eating quietly.

"So, have you guys found out the sex of the baby?" Mrs. Chris asked.

"No, Poetry wants it to be a surprise. As long as the baby is healthy, I really don't care what it is."

"Speaking of the baby," Poetry said, jumping up. She went to the coffee table in the living room and grabbed something from her purse. "I thought you may want a copy of this."

She handed her mama two sonogram pictures and the tears flowed. "Aww! Monty you cursed my grandbaby with a big ass head." We all laughed at her joke. She wasn't lying, though. I did have a big head.

After dinner, we sat in front of the tree and sang Christmas carols. The thug nigga I was, I was rapping that shit, making everyone cry laughing. My phone rang and I pulled it from my hip. It was Jonathan.

"Excuse me, I have to take this. It's Jonathan," I said, standing up and walking across the room. "What up, man?"

"We found out where Dray lives. I've had a few people sitting on his place, but he hasn't showed up. Kaymee told me about a female named Alexis. I went and found her myself and the things she told me was crazy. If given the chance, he is going to hurt my baby. He has to be found and dealt with. Is there anyone else that you would know his whereabouts?

"Yeah, he's having a baby with a chick named Melody. She lives on thirty-three Trinity Avenue Southwest, apartment two B. I'm quite sure she has heard from him. Check it out and let me know what you find. Where is Kaymee?"

"She went somewhere with Los. I'm not worried about her because she is with one of our own. Plus, I saw how he was checking her out on Thanksgiving. She's good. I already told him if he sees that nigga, to blow his shit back.," Jonathan said.

"You told him right. I don't care what time it is, call me, Jay."

"Man, enjoy your time away. Hopefully this shit will be taken care of when you get back. I'll holla at you, though," he said, hanging up.

I joined my future wife and in laws by the tree and her mother suggested opening gifts. Majority of the gifts were for our baby that hadn't even made it into the world yet. It was good to know her parents were supporting us during this pregnancy.

"Thanks for the gifts. We'll figure out a way to get them to Atlanta," Poetry said, hugging both of her parents.

"This one is for you," her mama said, handing her a small wrapped box.

Poetry tore the wrapper off and opened the lid of the box. Inside there was a platinum chain with a platinum heart locket. When she opened the locket, there was a baby hospital picture of her in the inside. The other side of the locket was empty.

"That is your first photo, I want you to put the baby's photo on the other side. I thought it could be something that you would cherish forever," her mama explained.

"I love it! That was so thoughtful of you. I would've never thought to do something like this. Thank you!"

"You're welcome, baby," her mama said, giving her a hug. "Monty this is for you. I didn't know what to buy, but I hope you like it."

I took the gift from her and opened it. There was a Chicago Bears jersey inside. When I turned the Jersey around, it was customized with the words, 'First time Dad' and the number 1. I thought it was pretty cool and I loved the concept.

"Thank you so much! This dope!" I beamed.

"I'm glad you like it. Stan picked the shirt and I added the finishing touches," she said.

"Yeah, I thought it was cheesy as hell, but you like it," Stan said, laughing.

Poetry and I gave her mama a five-hundred-dollar Visa gift card because we didn't know what kind of gift to get her. We bought her dad season tickets for the Chicago Bears next football season. I earned a couple more brownie points from him with that gift.

"I appreciate everything y'all have done. I love you both," she said to her parents. I'm tired, so I'm going upstairs to lay down. Monty, would you help clean up?" she asked as I helped her stand up. I shook my head yes and grabbed her hand to help her up the stairs. "I'll be fine. You don't have to come up with me, babe," she said, kissing me deeply.

"We love you too, Pumpkin," Stan said.

When she disappeared, Mrs. Chris looked at me sadly and said, "Take care of my baby, Monty."

"I will," was all I could muster up to say back.

By the time we finished cleaning up the wrapping paper, the kitchen, and taking the baby gifts in the guest room down the hall, I was tired myself. But Stan and I stayed down stairs talking and smoking until he turned in for the night.

Chapter 22
Kaymee

Staying at my dad's was the best decision I could've made. With Dray still on the loose, I was a nervous wreck at times. My face had healed well and there weren't any traces of the bruises. Carlos had been there for me the whole way through. At first, I didn't want anything to do with him, but he ignored all of my rejections.

We went out yesterday which was Christmas Eve and have been texting ever since he dropped me off. Jumping into another relationship wasn't something I wanted to do, but I don't want him to think it's more than it actually was. I was sitting in my room waiting for my daddy to come back from taking care of business when my phone chimed.

I smiled as I picked it up because I knew it wasn't anyone but Carlos. I opened the text message and there was a text from a number I didn't know. Curiosity got the best of me and I opened it.

470-555-8825: I bet you thought I was gon' go away forever, didn't you? I may not be in plan sight, but I see everything. Don't get that nigga fucked up. BTW, Merry Christmas.

My hands shook as I held the phone. I blocked Dray, now he was calling me from another number. He was watching me and I didn't know when nor where. I was scared, but I had to convince him to think everything was okay between us.

Me: Merry Christmas, Dray. Who are you talking about fucking up?

I wanted to see if he really knew who I'd been out with. Knowing him, he was only speculating because he hasn't been seen around lately. It didn't take him too long to respond back.

470-555-8825: Don't play dumb with me! You know exactly who I'm talking about.

Dray didn't know shit about what I was doing or who I was doing it with. He was trying to trip me up and I was ready to play his game. I was tired of him thinking he owned me and would live my life in fear.

Me: Where are you, Dray?

470-555-8825: Why are you changing the subject?

Me: There is no man that you could possibly be talking about. My face just cleared up from you punching the fuck out of me! Who would want me other than you? Now again, where are you? I want to see you.

Dray didn't respond after I said that. Hopefully he felt guilty about what he had done to me. I turned on the TV and started watching *Law and Order: Special Victims Unit.* The episode was getting good when my phone chimed and it was Dray again.

470-555-8825: I was just testing you. I'm out of town on business. Seeing me is not going to happen no time soon. Tell yo' daddy I'll get his money to him when I get back in a couple months.

Me: A couple months! Dray you know you have to give him his money sooner than that to avoid any problems.

470-555-8825: He'll get it when I give it to him! Just tell him what I said!

Me: You have his number. Call him yourself. I'm not getting in that. You still haven't told me where you are.

470-555-8825: I'm not stupid. You are trying to find out where I am for Jonathan! You don't know where I am, but I know where you are. Keep looking good and don't let your guard down. I still love you, but I hate that you just tried to set me up.

Me: Set you up? What the hell are you talking about? I was asking where you were, nothing more.

Dray didn't text me back, so I picked up the phone and called Jonathan. I made a promise to let him know if Dray contacted me at any time. Whatever plan they had for him was fine by me.

"Hey, baby girl. What's going on?"

"Dray just texted me and I wanted to give you the number he used. He didn't call from his number," I explained.

"Kaymee, forward me the entire text thread. I need to read them myself. Did he say he was still in Atlanta?"

"I'm sending them now and nope, he said he was out of town on business."

"Out of town on business, my ass! That nigga ran and he is gon' die for putting his hands on you and for running with my shit. If he contacts you again, let me know. I'll be back home in about an hour. Merry Christmas, Kaymee," he said, hanging up.

Before I could put my phone down, it started ringing. It was Poetry. I hurriedly answered, "Merry Christmas, sis!" I screamed into the phone.

"Mee, you know damn well you can't be hollering in my ear," she said, laughing. "Merry Christmas to you, too. Did you get the gift I left for you in your top drawer of your night stand?" she asked.

"What gift? I haven't even been in there!" I said, rolling over and opening the drawer.

As she said, there was a small box wrapped in shiny green wrapping paper. The label read, 'To my best friend /sister, from the only sister you have' with a smiley face.

"Aww, Poe! I should've given you your gift before you left!" I said as I tore the paper off.

Opening the box, there was a picture of the two of us that was in a picture frame that read, 'Best friends for life.' In the picture, we were hugging each other tightly after we graduated high school. That was a time to remember because that was the day we knew we had made it.

"Thank you very much! I will treasure this picture like I treasure our friendship. I love you, Poe," I said with tears in my eyes.

"That's not all. There's another box on the top shelf of your closet," she said, laughing.

"You play too much, sis!" I said, hopping up from the bed and racing to the closet. The box was big and I was excited. I placed the box on the bed and put the phone on speaker. "What's in this big ass box, Poe?"

"Open it and see, fool!"

When I got the paper off, there was a Builder Bear staring up at me. It had on a pair of black jeans, a green, black, and white jersey jacket, with my name stitched on the front. It also had on a pair of green and white Chucks. I started laughing and fell on top of the box. "Poe, why did you buy this bear for me? I told you I was going back to get it the next time we was out."

"I wanted to get it and add a special touch to it. Take it out the box and push the hand. There's a message waiting for you to listen to." The smile could be heard in her voice.

"Omg! I love it as I removed the bear from the box. As I held the bear in my arm, I picked up the phone so Poetry could listen with me. I pushed the button and Poetry's voice filled the room.

"Merry Christmas, sis! I wanted you to know you mean everything to me. No matter what happens, you will forever

be in my heart. It will always be just you and me. I love you."

The recording ended with her making a kiss sound and the tears cascaded down my face. I couldn't say anything for a couple minutes because I was trying to figure out the hidden message behind what she said. There's a reason for everything, but I didn't want to express what I was feeling.

"Thank you so much. I love it and I love you, too. Hurry and come back so we can have some fun before you drop that load," I said, wiping my face.

"I'll be back Saturday morning. Monty and I are leaving tonight to head to Vegas. Did he tell you anything about this trip, Mee?"

I wasn't about to spoil Montez's surprise that he had set up for her. It's been a long time coming and I was glad she opened the door for him to put it into play. I hated lying to her, but this was one lie I wouldn't regret.

"No, I don't know what he has planned for y'all. I want to hear all about it though. As a matter of fact, take lots of pictures because I want to see what Vegas is about. One day we will go back together,"

"I will. Enough about me, what's new with you?" she asked.

"Dray texted me today and he tried to say he saw me with somebody. I got scared because I thought he was watching me again. I asked him where he was and he accused me of trying to set him up. I passed all the information to my daddy so he could take care of it."

"Dray needs to enjoy his life while he can. He fucked up on all levels and there's no coming back from it. Wherever he is, he better stay there and never return to Atlanta. Fuck Dray, tell me about Los."

"Poe, there's nothing to tell about Los. We are just friends, nothing more. We went out yesterday and had a good time. That's all."

"Has he called since he left you?" she asked, being nosy.

"Yes, I've talked to him several times. What are you getting at, Poe?"

"I want you to live your life! Don't let anything hold you back. There's nothing wrong with getting to know him. Take things slow but don't block out the possibility."

"I'm definitely going to keep an open mind with Carlos. I also have to remember, Dray started out the same way. I don't need a repeat of the drama that's still going on in my life." Poetry spoke Carlos up because he was calling on the other line. "Poe, let me call you right back. Carlos is calling now," I said, smiling.

"Okay, sis. I'll talk to you later," she said, hanging up.

I caught the call before the voicemail picked up. "Hello."

"Hey, Kaymee. I was just calling to see how you were doing. Merry Christmas," Los said.

"Merry Christmas to you, too! I'm doing alright. Sitting here watching TV, waiting on my daddy to come back. What are you doing on this Christmas day?" I asked.

"Right now, I'm sitting around watching football with my family. I'll be going out later to work a little bit. I know you told me not to buy anything, but I had to. I won't force you to accept it, but I'll have it for you whenever you're ready."

"Carlos, you have been here for me since the incident at Walmart and I appreciate it so much. The last thing I want to do is lead you on. All I can guarantee at this moment is friendship, nothing more. I hope you understand the position I'm in right now."

"Kaymee, that's fine. I'm not the type of nigga that forces a female to do anything. Do I like you? Yes, I do. I also know that you were in a toxic relationship and was mentally damaged by it. I figured I'd get you out to enjoy life instead of moping around in the house blaming yourself for what happened. None of that was your fault. I will do whatever it takes to keep that pretty smile on your face. I didn't want anything really. I had to check on you," he said.

"Thank you for calling. I'll talk to you soon."

I laid down with my Bear and continued watching TV with Poetry on my mind. The eerie way I was feeling wouldn't go away and I didn't know the meaning behind it. Pressing the button on the bear, I listened to her voice over and over and drifted off to sleep.

Chapter 23
Poetry

The joy I felt spending time with my parents was what I needed. I really missed being home, but I had moves to make on my own. Monty was there getting closer to both of them and that made me smile too because they made me realize he was the one for me. I've finally come to terms he'd made a mistake with the decision to mess around with Mena. I couldn't hold it over his head any longer.

We left Chicago at seven and arrived in Vegas at five thirty. There was a two-hour time difference and I knew after a while, I would be tired as hell. Arriving at the Venetian Resort, I was amazed at how beautiful the hotel was. When we entered the suite that Montez had reserved, my breath was taken away.

There was an open bedroom that overlooked a living room. Walking into the bathroom, there was a hug tub separating the glass-enclosed shower and the double sinks. I didn't have to worry about fighting with Montez about hogging the sink.

Sitting on the bed, I almost passed out it was so comfortable. Montez brought our bags in and walked over to where I had laid back on the bed. He lifted my foot and removed my shoes and massaged each one before he picked me up and carried me to the shower. He undressed me and turned the shower on before helping me inside.

I let the water fall on my back as he undressed and stepped in behind me. Montez washed me from head to toe and rinsed my body. "I love you, Poetry Renee'," he said, kissing my shoulders as he rubbed my stomach.

"I love you too, baby. I'm tired and need to take a nap. You can go downstairs and gamble for a couple hours if you want," I said, placing my hand on top of his.

"Nah, I'll stay and hold you until we get up to go to our appointment," he said, turning the water off.

"Appointment?" I asked curiously.

"Let me get you dried off and I'll tell you all about it," he said, exiting the shower.

The towel he held open for me was soft and warm. I couldn't help glancing down at his third leg as it hung looking like a log of dark chocolate. My kitty was trying to sing a song, but I was too tired for that shit. It wasn't happening.

After wrapping a towel around his waist, he opened the door and the steam followed us into the bedroom area. Montez helped me onto the bed and went to his luggage. He stayed bent down for a minute and it looked like he was praying. Bringing something to his lips, he stood and turned toward me with tears in his eyes.

"Poetry, I did some fucked up shit and lost you for months," he said, walking back to the bed. "It was the biggest mistake of my life. I've apologized about my actions and swore it would never happen again and I meant that. What I'm about to ask you is something I've been dreaming about for years. In my eyes, you have always been my wife. Today I want to make it official. Poetry Renee'—" he paused, dropping down on one knee with a ring box in his hand. "Will you marry me?" he asked, opening the box with tears falling down his face.

My hands covered my mouth and I couldn't utter a word. I looked at the ring and it was beautiful. His infidelities clouded my mind, but I remembered the talk I had with myself about completely forgiving him and pushing them out of my mind. I shook my head yes because I still couldn't find my voice.

"Is that a yes, future Mrs. Williams?"

"Yes, I will marry you, baby!" I said, throwing my hands around his neck. He stood up, taking the ring out of the box and slid it on my left ring finger. Montez kissed my lips and I deepened it when I slipped my tongue in his mouth. I pecked his lips once more and pulled back. "About that Mrs. Williams thing. I want to hyphenate my name. Parker got my daddy blood on it," I smirked.

"That's not a problem as long as your daddy knows that Montez Williams is your husband and he is your daddy. I don't think there would be any problems, though. Stan my nigga now," he said, laughing. "I'm ready to make you the happiest woman in the world, baby. Watch ya man turn your life into the fairytale you've always dreamed of." He kissed me again. "Now, get some rest so my baby will be well rested. We are hitting the town today, baby!"

Montez crawled into the bed and pulled me down beside him. We were snuggled against each other and sleep came pretty easy for me. The smile on my face stayed there until my breathing labored. I was happy that he wanted to marry me and I couldn't wait to become, Mrs. Poetry Renee' Parker-Williams.

***

Montez and I went to a small chapel on the strip and got married. It took less than an hour, but the love will last a lifetime. It was hot as hell even though it was late evening and I needed to go inside. We made our way to the Mandalay Bay Resort and Casino where Montez got us tickets to see Michael Jackson One, I loved me some MJ, but I was nervous about being at that hotel after the shooting that happened in 2017.

The show started in thirty minutes and we got drinks and food before we found our seats. I had seen little clips of the show on the internet but being there in the flesh was exciting. The lights went off and clips of Michael's video started playing on a screen hanging in the back of the stage. As the lights came on, the dancers were doing acrobatic stunts to the tunes of "Smooth Criminal".

I started clapping and singing along with the music as I struggled to keep my eyes on everything that was going on. My eyes focused on one dancer that was doing all the moves as the others, but on walking sticks because he only had one leg. That didn't stop him because he was getting down.

"Oh my gawd, baby! did you see that?" I leaned over and screamed in Montez's ear. He smiled at me and shook his head yes.

He was enjoying the show just as much as I was, but I was all into it like I was part of the show. The stunts that were being performed were spectacular. The performers had all the moves down packed and I was floored when they did Michael's infamous lean that he did in the video. I was having the time of my life and didn't want it to end.

Song after song, I was impressed. After the ninety-minute show, I wanted to see it again. I overexerted myself and was ready to hit the sack. We went out to eat and checked out the strip for a little while. It was almost midnight when I told my husband, I like how that sounds, LOL, that I was tired.

"Okay, baby. Let's get you back to the hotel so you can get your beauty rest."

"I really enjoyed myself with you today. Thank you for making this a Christmas to remember. I love you and I'm going to have to think about how to top this as a surprise to you," I said, hugging his waist.

"Don't try to compete with me, Poe. I'm two steps ahead of you. I'm gon' attack your heart every chance I get. The level of surprises I have in store for you can't be fucked with. I won't stop you from trying, though."

Waiting to cross the street to the hotel, a bus passed us and there was an entire group of naked women on the side of the bus as advertisement. I was shocked because there were plenty of kids out and about with their parents. I see now what the saying 'What happens in Vegas, stays in Vegas' was all about. I would never bring my child here because it's not a place for minors.

I couldn't believe I was a married woman, I thought looking at my ring. Monty and I entered the suite and I sat on the couch and took a picture of my ring. I sent it in a group text to my parents and Kaymee with the caption, "I's married nah! Poetry Renee' Parker-Williams"

"What are you over here doing woman?" Montez asked as he sat next to me.

"I just sent a picture of my ring to my parents and Mee. I hope they won't be mad at me for basically eloping," I said nervously.

"Don't worry about it. They would be happy for us."

"How are you so sure?" I asked.

"Poe, do you think I brought you here without talking to the people that means so much to you beforehand? You know me better than that. They already know. The only thing you did was showed your mom and Mee the ring. Your dad saw it on Christmas Eve when he gave me permission to marry his daughter."

Hearing him say that everyone was onboard with us getting married had me crying like a baby. My phone chimed and Kaymee was the first to respond.

Sis: That ring is beautiful! Congratulations to both of you!

Sis: Mrs. Williams has a nice ring to it. I'm happy for both of you!

Mom: Congrats, baby! I love that ring, Mrs. Parker-Williams! Tell Monty he just started some shit in my house because your ring looks better than mine.

Dad: I'm trying to sleep! And Monty I'm kicking your ass! Congrats, now go to bed!

Mom: Get ready to upgrade me, daddy.

Poetry: OMG, mom! Thanks y'all. I'm sorry daddy, but I wanted to share my excitement with you. I love y'all and Mee I'll see you Saturday.

I handed my phone to Montez and let him read the messages. He laughed hard and I got up and walked to the bedroom. I was ready to sleep. I heard more chimes from my phone, so I knew Montez were aggravating my dad by responding for himself. Washing my face and brushing my teeth, I went back to the bed and crawled underneath the sheets. The entire day's events were dancing in my head and it was the lullaby I needed to sleep like a baby.

Chapter 23
Montez

I was enjoying the life of being a married man. It made me think about life in general. Poetry and I were about to be parents and the life I was living as far as selling drugs, was something I wanted to change. I had enough money to live a great life for many years to come. It was time to invest into something that would generate plenty of revenue. Speaking to Jonathan about ideas was the best decision I'd ever made.

It was the middle of January and Poetry was now seven months pregnant and looked like she was ready to pop. I tried my best to keep her comfortable every chance I got. Her headaches were worse than before, so I stayed in with her so she wouldn't be alone. Kaymee was a huge help when I was out in the streets.

Coming in my apartment from another night of hustling and trying to find a spot for my soul food restaurant, I went straight to the bedroom to check on my wife. She and Kaymee where sleeping in the bed. I knew it was too late for her to go back to Jonathan's, so I went into the guest room and laid down.

Sometime later, I heard Poetry scream out, "I think my water just broke!" I jumped up and ran into our bedroom and flipped on the light. Kaymee was standing on the side of the bed and Poetry was looking under the covers at what I assumed was the wetness.

"Why are you still laying there, Poe? Get up so we can get to the hospital," I said, going to the closet to get the bag she had packed months ago. Throwing the bag on the foot of the bed, I ran to the other room to get my phone. "Yes, her water broke and I wanted to let you know that we are on our way to the hospital now." I was talking to Dr. Brim and racing back to the room. "Okay, we will see you soon."

Kaymee had helped Poetry get dressed and was tying her shoes. I grabbed the bag and helped her put her jacket on. It took everything in me not to pick her up and carry her to the car. Poetry jumped in the back seat with Poetry and I started the car and backed out of the parking spot. The police would have to chase my ass to the hospital because I wasn't stopping.

I parked in front of the hospital and hopped out. "You can't park there, sir," a male doctor shouted at me.

"Fuck what you talking about! My wife's water broke and I need a wheelchair! How about you go get one!" I didn't mean to scream at him, but I didn't have time for his bullshit. I helped Poetry out of the car and turned to Kaymee. "Park my shit, sis, before I have to fuck somebody up."

The doctor came back out with a wheelchair and we rushed inside. I told the nurse to let Kaymee back when she came in. We were escorted to Labor and Delivery and I was nervous as hell. Transferring her to the bed, the nurses helped Poetry put on a gown and hooked her up to machines to monitor the baby and start an IV.

When the nurses left the room, Poetry looked at me and said, "Get my phone and call my mama, bae." I did what she asked and passed the phone to her. "Hey, mommy. I'm in the hospital. I guess this baby is ready to make its grand entrance," she said, chuckling.

"How are you feeling, baby?" her mama asked in a shaky voice.

"My head is hurting, I'm feeling a little bit of pain, but other than that, I'm fine. I just wanted to let you know what was going on."

"You are going to be in the hospital, so they can keep an eye on you. Did your water break?"

"Yeah, it did."

"It's too soon for the baby to come. They will have you on bedrest. I'll let your dad know and we will be there as soon as we can. I love you, Poetry. Everything will be alright."

"I love you too, mama. Hurry up and get here," Poetry said as a tear rolled down the side of her head.

I didn't know why she was so emotional, but I knew her being sad wouldn't be good for the baby. I had to let her know I was going to be there every step of the way. Bending down, I kissed her on the lips and grabbed her by the hand. I entwined our hands and rubbed my thumb along the back of hers.

"I love you, baby. Women have babies every day and you will see our baby soon. There's nothing to cry about. We got this," I said, kissing her forehead.

Poetry closed her eyes and Dr. Brim came into the room. She checked the machines before she came over to the bed. Checking to make sure everything was connected properly, she sat on the side of the bed and gave Poetry a hug.

"You don't have anything to be worried about, Poetry. It's not uncommon for the water bag to break early. There are things on our end that we have to keep an eye on. I'm going to check your cervix to make sure everything is okay."

Dr. Brim had Poetry open her legs and placed the sheet on her knees so she could see. She put her gloved hand inside of Poetry and she winced a little bit. When Dr. Brim let her legs down and took the gloves off, she had a serious expression on her face.

"You are almost three centimeters, but it's too soon for the baby to come. I want to administer antibiotics to prevent infection as well as an injection of potent steroids called corticosteroids. That is used to mature the baby's lungs. I want to delay the delivery process long as possible. You are only twenty-nine weeks and I need you to be further along before I even think about delivering. That means you will be living here with us for a while. Are you up for that?" Dr. Brim asked, smiling.

"Why did this happen?" Montez asked Dr. Brim.

"From what I'm seeing, her blood pressure is elevated and it's been that way throughout her pregnancy. I'm paying close attention to keep it under control. We will make sure she gets the best care possible here," she explained.

"She's been complaining that her headaches are worse than before. What's that all about?" Monty was asking about everything that we've been concerned about since day one.

"It could be from her blood pressure, but we haven't been able to determine the cause as a whole. I will give her some pain killers through her IV and we will go from there. Get some rest, sweetie and I'll be back soon," Dr. Brim said, walking out the door.

***

Everything was going well and we had been in the hospital for a week. We made it to week thirty and I was happy. Poetry's parents were in Atlanta and Kaymee damn near lived in the hospital with us. Jonathan and Katrina came to check on us and even G and the other Goons came down to support along with their wives. This is what I say about family. Everyone was there to make sure Poetry had mad love in that hospital.

Kaymee and the ladies had left earlier and me and Poetry were alone watching Tyler Perry movies. Her laughter filled the room with every joke told and I sucked it all up. About an hour later, the door opened and everyone filed in bearing gifts. Both Poetry and I were surprised and wanted to know what was going on.

"What the hell is all of this?" I asked stunned.

"We didn't have a baby shower, so I figured we would bring it to y'all. Teetee's baby can't come into this world without us giving a party!" Kaymee said.

"Yeah, I agree," Nova, G's wife chimed in. "I didn't come all the way from the Windy City and not celebrate with you, nephew. Poetry deserves to have a shower."

Poetry was so emotional, the tears were flowing down her cheeks. There were cases of pampers in all sizes, onesies, socks, t-shirts, and outfits all in neutral colors. G bought a bracelet for the baby that said 'daddy's girl' because he was sure we were having a girl. He had Jade on his side because she bought a bunch of pink shit, too. I hope they saved the receipts because my son was not wearing pink nothing. I didn't give a damn what these niggas was wearing out there in the world.

"I didn't have time to shop. Do I look like a shopping nigga? Y'all better take this envelope and be happy with the shit," Scony said, handing it to Poetry.

We had a good time laughing and talking shit. They brought grape juice and little finger foods that Poetry could eat. Everyone stayed until Poetry clunked out and fell asleep. I sat watching her for a while until G and Jonathan told me to take a walk with them. Kaymee laid back on the sofa bed with her feet in Los' lap and I knew my baby was good. We went outside and sat in G's truck to blow something. Lawd, knew I needed it.

"Is everything good, brah?" G asked.

"So far so good. I'm worried about the headaches that she keeps having. We've been battling this shit since the day we found out about her pregnancy. I don't know what the fuck is up, but I hope they find out after she has the baby. There's plenty of tests that couldn't be ran because of her being pregnant."

"Well, at least ya'll are on top of it. If there's anything you need, all you have to do is call. I received a couple of emails about a few spots. I'm doing what is needed to get you out of the game so you can do what you have to for your family. When I eat, we all eat, so we are gon' always be good in this family," Jonathan said.

"I appreciate everything you are doing and thank you for understanding what I want to do. It's not about me anymore. I have to live on the straight and narrow for my seed and my wife."

"You don't have to thank me because I'm here to make sure you good on all levels. That's what it's about," Jonathan said without hesitation.

"Same goes for me. When we find that nigga Dray, I got that on lock," G said.

"Nah, when y'all find that muthafucka, I want in. I got a promise I have to fulfill on his ass." We all laughed. "Thank y'all for bringing joy into that room today."

"That had nothing to do with us, them damn women did that shit and *told* us we better participate," G said, shaking his head.

"Well I'll have to thank the sister clan then because y'all made her day."

"We just wanted to get you out for a minute to get some air and kush in yo' lungs. We're about to blow this joint, but we'll holla at ya later," Jonathan said, getting out of the truck.

We hugged up and I headed back into the hospital.

***

Poetry and I was playing Uno while Kaymee slept. I was whooping her ass, taking all her cranberry juice boxes that she had the nurses stealing for her. Hitting her with a draw four, then a draw two three times, a skip, reverse and went out. She was mad as hell.

"Monty, you cheated!" she screamed, poking her lip out.

"Awww, baby. Don't be a sore loser. I won fair and square." She wasn't trying to hear none of what I was saying.

"Don't talk to me, Monty," she said, turning her back to me.

We had made it to week thirty-three and we were almost there. Poetry was tired of being in the hospital, but she didn't have a choice but to sit back and wait for the show. She thought I was about to let her be mad over a game, but she was crazy. I put the cards away and got in the bed behind her.

"Come here, Pookie," I said, kissing the back of her neck. "You know I loves me some you. I'll let you win next time. Fuck that! You winnin' now because you are Mrs. Williams in this bitch! Now turn around and give me some lips."

She turned around and melted in my arms. I kissed her like my life depended on it. Her tongued tasted like the cranberries I had beat her for. Of course I wasn't going to take her funky juice, but she didn't know that. We laid tangled up for the rest of the night before I got up to use the bathroom.

I was draining my hose when I heard the machines going off like crazy. I pissed upside the wall as I whipped around to listen. Barely getting my joint back into my pants, I was out of the bathroom like lightening. Dr. Brim and nurses were in the room and I instantly got scared.

"What's going on?" I screamed. No one responded to my question. "What happened?" I asked, pushing my way through the nurses to get to Poetry.

"Step back, Mr. Williams! The baby's heart rate has dropped dangerously low! We must get her to the operating room now!" Dr. Brim screamed back at me.

I couldn't see her as they unlocked the wheels on the bed and rolled her out of the room. Kaymee was sitting motionless on the sofa bed as I headed out of the room behind my wife. "Call her parents!" I screamed over my shoulder.

As I followed the crowd to the operating room, Dr. Brim had a nurse to direct me to a room to get scrubbed up and dressed in a gown. I tried to do it as fast as possible so I could be by Poetry's side. When I got in the room, they had already administered the anesthesia and Dr. Brim was already making the incision.

Sitting on the stool next to Poetry's head, I noticed that she looked pale in color. She had tears in her eyes and she turned her head, looking at me. There was something different about her, but I didn't know what it was.

"Montez Williams, I love you so much. I'm sorry for wasting so much time, fighting you for the mistake that separated us for months. Please forgive me, baby," she said, closing her eyes.

"Baby, that's behind us. Don't worry about it. I love you, too. We have the rest of our lives to make memories."

I grabbed her hand and she squeezed it tightly. Looking up to see what was happening on the other side of the divider, I still felt the grip Poetry had on my hand. Dr. Brim had both of her hands inside Poetry's belly and when she came out with my baby, the cord was wrapped around its neck. One of the nurses grabbed the baby while Dr. Brim untangled the cord, freeing my baby girl.

She was immediately taken to a baby bed and given oxygen. The minute the baby started crying, Poetry's grip loosened and her hand dropped. The heart monitor started buzzing and the line was going flat by the second.

All I heard was, "Code Blue!" and my mind went blank.

To Be Continued…
Love Shouldn't Hurt 4
Coming Soon

Submission Guideline

Submit the first three chapters of your completed manuscript to ldpsubmissions@gmail.com, subject line: Your book's title. The manuscript must be in a .doc file and sent as an attachment. Document should be in Times New Roman, double spaced and in size 12 font. Also, provide your synopsis and full contact information. If sending multiple submissions, they must each be in a separate email.

Have a story but no way to send it electronically? You can still submit to LDP/Ca$h Presents. Send in the first three chapters, written or typed, of your completed manuscript to:

LDP: Submissions Dept
Po Box 870494
Mesquite, Tx 75187

DO NOT send original manuscript. Must be a duplicate.

Provide your synopsis and a cover letter containing your full contact information.

Thanks for considering LDP and Ca$h Presents.

Coming Soon from Lock Down Publications/Ca$h Presents

BOW DOWN TO MY GANGSTA

By **Ca$h**

TORN BETWEEN TWO

By **Coffee**

BLOOD STAINS OF A SHOTTA **III**

By **Jamaica**

STEADY MOBBIN **III**

By **Marcellus Allen**

BLOOD OF A BOSS **V**

By **Askari**

LOYAL TO THE GAME **IV**

LIFE OF SIN II

By **T.J. & Jelissa**

A DOPEBOY'S PRAYER **II**

By **Eddie "Wolf" Lee**

IF LOVING YOU IS WRONG… **III**

LOVE ME EVEN WHEN IT HURTS **II**

By **Jelissa**

TRUE SAVAGE **VI**

By **Chris Green**

BLAST FOR ME **III**

A BRONX TALE III

DUFFLE BAG CARTEL

By **Ghost**

ADDICTIED TO THE DRAMA **III**

By **Jamila Mathis**

LIPSTICK KILLAH **III**

WHAT BAD BITCHES DO **III**

KILL ZONE **II**

By **Aryanna**

THE COST OF LOYALTY **II**

By **Kweli**

SHE FELL IN LOVE WITH A REAL ONE **II**

By **Tamara Butler**

RENEGADE BOYS **III**

By **Meesha**

CORRUPTED BY A GANGSTA **IV**

By **Destiny Skai**

A GANGSTER'S CODE **III**

By **J-Blunt**

KING OF NEW YORK IV

RISE TO POWER II

By **T.J. Edwards**

GORILLAS IN THE BAY II

De'Kari

THE STREETS ARE CALLING II

Duquie Wilson

KINGPIN KILLAZ III

Hood Rich

STEADY MOBBIN' **III**

Marcellus Allen

SINS OF A HUSTLA II

ASAD

CASH MONEY HOES

Nicole Goosby

TRIGGADALE II

Elijah R. Freeman

MARRIED TO A BOSS 2…

By Destiny Skai & Chris Green

Available Now

RESTRAINING ORDER **I & II**

By **CA$H & Coffee**

LOVE KNOWS NO BOUNDARIES **I II & III**

By **Coffee**

RAISED AS A GOON I, II, III & IV

BRED BY THE SLUMS I, II, III

BLAST FOR ME I & II

ROTTEN TO THE CORE I III

A BRONX TALE I, II

By **Ghost**

LAY IT DOWN **I & II**

LAST OF A DYING BREED

BLOOD STAINS OF A SHOTTA I & II

By **Jamaica**

LOYAL TO THE GAME

LOYAL TO THE GAME II

LOYAL TO THE GAME III

LIFE OF SIN

By **TJ & Jelissa**

BLOODY COMMAS I & II

SKI MASK CARTEL I II & III

KING OF NEW YORK I II,III

RISE TO POWER

By **T.J. Edwards**

IF LOVING HIM IS WRONG…I & II

LOVE ME EVEN WHEN IT HURTS

By **Jelissa**

WHEN THE STREETS CLAP BACK I & II III

By **Jibril Williams**

A DISTINGUISHED THUG STOLE MY HEART I II & III

LOVE SHOULDN'T HURT I II III

RENEGADE BOYS I & II

By **Meesha**

A GANGSTER'S CODE I & II

By J-Blunt

PUSH IT TO THE LIMIT

By **Bre' Hayes**

BLOOD OF A BOSS **I, II, III & IV**

By **Askari**

THE STREETS BLEED MURDER **I, II & III**

THE HEART OF A GANGSTA I II& III

By **Jerry Jackson**

TRUE SAVAGE II

TRUE SAVAGE **III**

TRUE SAVAGE **IV**

TRUE SAVAGE **V**

By **Chris Green**

A DOPEBOY'S PRAYER

By **Eddie "Wolf" Lee**

THE KING CARTEL **I, II & III**

By **Frank Gresham**

THESE NIGGAS AIN'T LOYAL **I, II & III**

By **Nikki Tee**

GANGSTA SHYT **I II &III**

By **CATO**

THE ULTIMATE BETRAYAL

By **Phoenix**

BOSS'N UP **I , II & III**

By **Royal Nicole**

I LOVE YOU TO DEATH

By Destiny J

I RIDE FOR MY HITTA

I STILL RIDE FOR MY HITTA

By **Misty Holt**

LOVE & CHASIN' PAPER

By **Qay Crockett**

TO DIE IN VAIN

SINS OF A HUSTLA

By **ASAD**

BROOKLYN HUSTLAZ

By **Boogsy Morina**

BROOKLYN ON LOCK I & II

By **Sonovia**

GANGSTA CITY

By **Teddy Duke**

A DRUG KING AND HIS DIAMOND I & II III

A DOPEMAN'S RICHES

HER MAN, MINE'S TOO I, II

By Nicole Goosby

TRAPHOUSE KING **I II & III**

KINGPIN KILLAZ

By **Hood Rich**

LIPSTICK KILLAH **I, II**

CRIME OF PASSION I & II

By **Mimi**

STEADY MOBBN' **I, II**

By **Marcellus Allen**

WHO SHOT YA **I, II**

Renta

GORILLAZ IN THE BAY

DE'KARI

TRIGGADALE

Elijah R. Freeman

GOD BLESS THE TRAPPERS I, II, III

THESE SCANDALOUS STREETS I, II, III

FEAR MY GANGSTA I, II, III

THESE STREETS DON'T LOVE NOBODY I, II

Tranay Adams

THE STREETS ARE CALLING

Duquie Wilson

MARRIED TO A BOSS…

By Destiny Skai & Chris Green